JUNGLE QUEST

by
Megan Stine
and
H. William Stine

Programming by Susan M. Zakar

A Parachute Press Book

SCHOLASTIC INC.
New York Toronto London Auckland Sydney Tokyo

Designed by Gene Siegel

ISBN 0-590-33166-3

12 11 10 9 8 7 6 5 4 3 2   5 6 7 8 9/8

Printed in the U. S. A.   01

Warning: The following information is crucial to the success of your mission. Read it carefully. It may save your life.

As a certified member of ACT (the Adventure Connection Team), your job, as always, is to defend the cause of good against evil. It won't be easy, because BRUTE (the Bureau of Random Unlawful Terror and Evil, an international organization bent on wreaking havoc throughout the world), will be fighting you every step of the way. Your computer expertise will be vital to this mission. So turn on your home system. Throughout this adventure you'll be called upon to program it to get the ACT team out of some really tough spots.

Look for the box chart next to the program instructions. It will tell you which micros will run each program. If the program won't run as is on your computer, consult the Reference Manual in the back of the book — fast! Good luck. This message will be erased from memory in 30 seconds.

CHAPTER
1

Friday afternoon — the best day of the week! The school bell sounds and you are free to do what you want for the next two days. But there's something in your locker that is going to change all of that. It's an envelope taped to the inside of your locker door. When you see it, you know that it can only come from one place — the official headquarters of the Adventure Connection Team in Washington, D.C. And it can only mean one thing. They want you for another mission NOW!

Standard Friday afternoon procedure, you think. Normally an ACT communication would come in on your computer terminal at home. But ACT knows you — there's no way you'd head straight home on Friday. The at-risk envelope just had to be used.

You're dying to know what the mission is, but you're only too aware of the dangers of trying to open an ACT communication without following proper identification procedures. The envelope, you, and probably half the school would be blown to a fine powder. So you put the envelope in your backpack and head for home as fast as you can.

Who ever thought that mailing in an ad coupon from a computer magazine would lead to this? Here you are — the ACT team's computer expert — traveling from country to country, even from planet to planet, helping to defeat enemies that no regular army or government agency could even imagine.

As you ride your bike onto your block, you see a bunch of the neighborhood kids crowded around a Mr. Smoothie Ice Cream truck. But you don't have time for that now — you jump off your bike and race into your room. In a second you've got your computer up and running. You tear open the ACT envelope and remove a folded sheet of red paper. The message is scrambled, of course. But your computer will soon take care of that.

GFWHQEA WGYZTW XHYLGZN.
PJWGQFNVRKF UAK GOLXVF.
EMFVWZFTV HOVMFU IFLMYDYKW
GQFKMFKVV.
GQGJ MOKQD 48 HIG NFXN!
YMJBG HOALVZXZUH 5 MKAUGUA.

You rummage through a stack of recent comic books — there it is! The latest issue of Marvel's *X Men*. By placing a special transparency over the last page, you're able to read a secret BASIC program and this month's password — TOPAZ. That's all you need to decode the Red Alert.

Type the following program into your computer, and run it. Then enter the password and the coded message, in capital letters, one line at a time. Line 50 should be typed as one line on your computer.

PROGRAM 1

```
10  REM ENCODER/DECODER
20  P$ = " "
30  PRINT "ENTER YOUR PASSWORD"
40  INPUT K$
50  PRINT "TYPE EACH LINE OF SECRET
    MSG"
60  PRINT "(TYPE 'STOP' WHEN DONE)"
70  INPUT C$
80  IF C$ = "STOP" THEN 270
90  FOR I = 1 TO LEN(C$)
100 I$ = MID$(C$,I,1)
110 IF (I$ > = "A") * (I$ < = "Z") THEN 140
120 P$ = P$ + I$
130 GOTO 230
140 J = J + 1
150 IF J < = LEN(K$) THEN 170
```

```
160  J = 1
170  K = ASC(MID$(K$,J,1)) — ASC("A") + 1
180  C = ASC(I$) — ASC("A") + 1
190  IF K > C THEN 210
200  K = K + 26
210  P = K — C
220  P$ = P$ + CHR$(P + ASC("A") — 1)
230  NEXT I
240  PRINT P$
250  P$ = " "
260  GOTO 70
270  END
```

IBM	Apple		Radio Shack		Commodore		TI	Atari
PC & PCjr	II +	IIe	TRS-80	Color	64	VIC-20	99/4A	400/800
✓	✓	✓	✓	✓	✓	✓		

This program will run on all the personal computers checked in the chart above. See the Reference Manual, page 116, for changes for TI and Atari.

Five minutes!!?? Suddenly you're in fast forward, gathering up your miniature computer pack and all of the other equipment you need. Outside, a truck horn beeps three times —

that's the signal. Your ride to the secret ACT airport is waiting.

But on the street there are two trucks now, the Mr. Smoothie truck and a dark-blue van a few hundred feet behind. Which one is it? Check out the blue van, you decide. You angle across the street, but just as your hand reaches for the door, the ice-cream truck beeps again.

Close one! you think to yourself, sprinting back to Mr. Smoothie and sticking your head through the window.

"How you doin', Hot Wheels?" you say.

"Hey — stick to the rules," Hot Wheels says. "Code name?"

"Orion," you answer and slide in on the passenger side.

"Good to see you again," Hot Wheels says. "But hold on. We're in a hurry."

"What's the matter? Is your ice cream melting?" you ask as a joke.

"No, we've got company. That blue van has been following me and I don't think they're interested in my fudgie bars," the driver says, wheeling the truck in and out of lanes.

The ice-cream truck suddenly screeches and turns around and speeds down a new street.

"Did you lose the blue van?" you ask.

"They're still there. Either they're real good or they want you real bad, Orion. Scared?" Hot Wheels asks.

"I've been down this road before," you say. "But never this fast!"

"I'm going to let them catch up with us and when they do, toss a couple of those sundae bars at them," he says.

Did he just say what you think he said???

"Just be sure to pull the sticks out first," Hot Wheels adds as he watches the blue van pull alongside. "Now!!"

You pull out the sticks and toss the sundae bars at the truck. Splat! Splat! Two direct hits!! A thick, gooey mass quickly spreads over the truck and then begins to harden, slowing the truck to a crawl. When the stuff hardens completely, the truck is rooted to the street like a tree.

Minutes later, Hot Wheels drives onto a hidden airport runway where a jet is waiting to take off.

"Do you know why we're allowed to tell each other only our code names, Orion?" Hot Wheels asks as you get out of the truck.

"Yeah. Because in this line of work, it's too dangerous to know our real identities."

"Be careful out there, Orion," Hot Wheels says.

You and Hot Wheels shake hands quickly. Soon you're 20,000 feet in the sky and climbing — and you still don't know where you're going.

CHAPTER
2

The jet has just begun to level off at 30,000 feet, when the video screen at the front of the cabin snaps to life and brings you a live, remote broadcast from Mark Huntington, coordinator of ACT missions. All five people on board snap to life as well.

"Good afternoon, team," he says. "I'm glad to see you all made it. We've got a hairy one for you this time." Click . . . a photograph of a man's face comes on the screen.

"This is Professor Max Ballaster," Huntington continues. "Ballaster is an archaeologist, and for years he's been looking for a hidden temple wi . . ." *Crackle!* ". . . dol in it . . ." *Crackle, crackle. Buzzzzzzzzz.* In the middle of his speech, Mark Huntington's face suddenly turns to static and video snow. His voice cuts in and out for a second and then the picture goes dead.

At first the five of you on the jet just look around at each other. Besides you there is a young man wearing blue jeans and a Grateful Dead T-shirt; a woman in khaki safari clothes; a man in a wrinkled tan suit and wearing gold wire glasses; and finally there is a young black man who is sitting by himself in the back of the plane. He didn't say anything to anyone before the plane took off and you wonder if he will now.

"We might as well introduce ourselves," says the man in the wrinkled suit. "Code name: Digger. Occupation: Archaeologist. I have no idea what I'm doing on this mission but if it has anything to do with Max Ballaster, I regret coming already."

"What's that supposed to mean?" says the guy in the T-shirt. "Wait a minute — let me introduce myself before mouthing off. My code name is Erda, and I'm your dancing instructor. Just kidding. I'm an expert on the environment and I've been getting some atmospheric readings coming from Africa that twisted my needles! By all indications, the ozone layer is about to skip town. When I called headquarters they told me to hustle over here right away. Now what do you know about this Professor Ballaster, Digger?"

"Half the scientific community thinks the man's a joke — the other half hasn't made up its mind yet," Digger says.

Digger hasn't said much, but already it's pretty clear to you which group he falls into.

"For years," Digger says, "Ballaster's been talking about an extraterrestrial civilization. According to him these visitors from another planet colonized Earth centuries ago, on the African continent. When they left, they left behind them a relic, some kind of a statue guarding a hidden temple. Ballaster thinks this statue might be the source of an undiscovered and incredibly powerful form of energy."

"Well, that explains why I'm here," says the woman in khaki. "I'm a nuclear engineer and my code name is Celeste. Huntington, that jerk, didn't brief me and now I think I know why. If we're walking into some kind of an energy force time bomb, I'm the one who'll have to defuse it."

"And what about you?" Erda says, looking straight at you.

"My code name is Orion," you say. "I'm a computer expert."

"Terrific," Erda says with a Mr. Joker laugh. "That'll come in real handy if we have time for a quick game of Pac-Man in the jungle."

You quickly switch on the portable microwave link to the ACT mainframe and punch in a few codes on your portable computer. You begin to read the printout aloud. "Code name: Erda. True name: Classified. Born in Pontiac, Michigan. Played piano since childhood. . . . Joined peace movement in the 1960's. . . . Became an environmental specialist. . . . Never learned to swim. . . . Allergic reactions: positive to penicillin; positive to eggs. . . .Should I go on?''

"I think you made your point," Celeste says, laughing.

"Yeah, I agree," Erda says. "Remind me never to ask someone out for a date without checking with you first.''

Just then the scratching, crackling sound of a video transmission makes you all turn toward the front of the cabin again. Mark Huntington's face reappears on the screen.

"Well, we'll try this one more time" — Huntington smiles — "and hope the transmission holds. I assume that during that interruption you've filled one another in on some of the details. So let me just get to the crucial points.

"Yesterday, Max Ballaster called ACT headquarters to arrange an urgent meeting. He said over the phone that he had found the statue and the power source and it was beyond his wildest dreams. This morning, just before our meeting, Ballaster was kidnapped by agents of BRUTE.''

"They're welcome to him," Digger says under his breath.

"Our psychological profile of Ballaster indicates that he will cave in under BRUTE's methods of interrogation. He'll tell them the location of the statue long before you get to him. So his mission is a race to find and secure the energy force before BRUTE does.''

"Sounds typically impossible," Erda says.

"How are we supposed to win that race when BRUTE has a huge head start?"

"The State Department has given us 48 hours to do this our way," Huntington says. "If we fail, they'll handle it their way — which means military involvement. I don't need to describe the international chaos that could result when world powers hear of this potential weapon. . . .

"On the floor in front of the cabin," Huntington says, "you'll find a cardboard tube. It contains an old sketch we found in Ballaster's office. Of course Ballaster had all of his recent photographic evidence with him when he was kidnapped this morning, so it's gone. Score another one for BRUTE.

"One more thing: No one has been designated as team leader. You'll have to make decisions as a group. But that shouldn't be a problem. After all, your survival is at stake."

On that cheery note, the coordinator signs off and the video screen goes blank.

"Let's take a look at that drawing," Erda says, reaching for the cardboard tube.

"Just a minute," Digger interrupts. "We haven't all introduced ourselves yet."

One by one you all turn toward the back of the jet and face the young black man who is still sitting by himself, watching the four of you with unblinking dark eyes. Finally he says something. "I do not have a code name. I am not one of you."

12

"Then you'd better tell us pretty quickly what you're doing on this jet," Celeste says.

The young man slowly gets out of his seat and walks to the front of the cabin. "I am here because I know where we are going," he says.

"And just where is that?" Digger asks.

But the young man ignores the question. He wants to tell things in his own time and way.

"My name is Olano and up until two hours ago I was a student at Purdue University. A typical student — studying when I had to, partying on the weekends, and cheering for the sports teams at the home games. Except, I guess I wasn't typical enough—maybe because I was not born in this country. I was born in Africa, in a region of the jungle called the Boranu. That's where we are going because that's where Professor Ballaster thought he'd find his hidden temple, and his statue, and his new energy source."

"And just what made him think that he'd find it there?" Digger asks.

"I guess you could say because I told him it was there," Olano says. "The professor gave a series of lectures at Purdue. Afterward, I told him about many of the tribal legends of the Boranu jungle — legends that have been passed down for centuries about a great statue with unimaginable power — an idol with one great eye that sees everything — that even sees into the hearts of people."

"And what did he say?" Erda asks.

"Just four words — and he kept saying them over and over: 'I have found it.' "

"I don't believe it," Digger says. "Have you seen it — actually seen the temple with your own eyes?"

"I didn't exactly have a lot of free time to devote to researching old tribal legends," Olano says. "Life is not easy in that territory."

"Do you believe it exists?" you ask, barely controlling your excitement.

"I almost hope it does not, Orion," Olano says. And for the first time he addresses an ACT member without a tone of anger.

"Why?" you ask.

"There are ancient stories of entire tribes, thousands of men, women, and children, being wiped out in a split second of vengeance by the power of this statue," he explains.

14

"Wow. What did they do to deserve that?" Erda asks.

"They entered the temple," Olano says.

No one says anything for a minute. Then Digger reaches for the cardboard tube that Erda is holding. Digger opens it up and removes a large drawing, unrolling it for everyone to see. It is a drawing of a massive temple carved into the side of a mountain. Vines and trees surround and cover it so that there appears to be no way into the temple — and worse, no way out. In front of the temple stands an ominous and hypnotizing statue. It looks somewhat like a person, but not like any person you've seen on this planet. It has a head, but no distinct features except for one large, oval eye. You feel yourself being pulled to your feet and walking closer to see the drawing better.

"I'll believe it when I see it," Digger says. But he is staring at the drawing just like everyone else.

"So you will serve as our guide through the area?" you ask Olano.

"Yes," he says. "Mr. Huntington is a very persuasive man. I explained to him that many tribes in the territory do not think kindly toward one who was born there and chose to leave. He explained to me that the lives of millions of people were in my hands and that my one small life really shouldn't matter that much. And I guess, in the end, I agreed."

With that, everyone falls silent. You settle back into your seat, pulling a blanket up over your legs so you can go to sleep. It's seven more hours of nonstop flight time, and this may be the only rest you get. But the image of that vine-covered temple is spinning through your head and you don't fall asleep for several hours.

At midnight your time, you're awakened by the familiar tone of the fasten-seat-belt sign, followed by the voice of the pilot over the jet's public address system.

"Get into your seats," he shouts. "My computer says we've got only 10 minutes of fuel left. We're going to go down like a ton of bricks!"

CHAPTER

4

There's no sign of panic on anyone's face as the team members scramble to connect their seat belts. Still, you can't help wondering if anyone else's heart is racing like yours. The jet is holding steady — no nose dive and no horrible silence of dead engines . . . not yet, anyway.

Instinctively you reach for your portable computer. Maybe — just maybe — the jet's onboard computers are wrong. Maybe you're not really out of fuel. It's a slim chance, but it's worth a try! You enter figures and miles and gallons quickly, without making a single mistake. For some reason your flying fingers don't know how scared the rest of you is.

But your computer printout removes any trace of hope. You're going to be out of fuel in minutes, just as the pilot said. So you start typing again furiously. You want to leave some kind of a message just in case someone finds the computer in the wreckage. But you get an error code — and then another. *That's strange,* you think. And suddenly you're getting nothing but error codes — no matter what you do.

"Something's wrong with my computer," you shout.

"Forget it," Erda shouts back. "You'll never get your money back after this trip."

"We've got less than a minute of fuel," the jet pilot says over the public address system. "I'm going to have to ditch her in the water. Get ready. . . ."

"Don't you get it?" you try again. "There was nothing wrong with my computer a little while ago. Something crazy's going on and it's messing up my computer."

Everyone looks at you as though you're worrying about the wrong thing at the wrong time. But you don't have a second to explain. You rush into the cockpit just as the plane starts to take a dive.

"Pull it up! Pull it up!! The computers are crazy!" you shout.

"Orion, the fuel's gone. I've got to start the descent now. The lower we are when the engines go out, the better our chances."

"Just wait 30 seconds — that's all," you tell him.

You can't tell what's going through the pilot's mind. You know he knows his aircraft — but in his heart, he must hope that you're right, because he waits, keeping the engines going full blast. Five seconds, then 10,

18

go by. Everyone in the cockpit waits for the engines to go silent. Twenty seconds go by — the engines are still going. Thirty seconds — there's no drop in power.

"We're going to make it," the pilot says, slowly removing his hand from the control that would have sent the jet crashing into the water.

"Hey, captain — look at this," the co-pilot says. "The computers are back up again. We've got plenty of fuel and everything else checks out A-OK, too."

The pilot turns back to you again and says, "I don't know what's going on down there — and I sure am glad I don't have to find out." He gives you a smile that you return — only you're not sure the joke is all that funny. You go back into the cabin.

"Well, is someone going to tell us what the devil's going on?" Digger asks.

"Everything's fine," you say. "We'll be over the drop in a couple minutes."

"Let's get our chutes on," Celeste says.

"But what happened up there? What about the fuel?" Erda asks.

"Computer error," you say, looking past Celeste and directly at Olano.

"Computer error??!" he laughs. "Well, don't feel bad, Orion. A couple of months ago, I got an electric bill for $12,000."

Everyone laughs at his joke — probably louder than they should have, but it's the only way to let the tension out. Then everyone starts to scramble into their parachutes and check out all the special equipment and tools they brought with them. Digger packs up a box of shovels and picks and brushes of all sizes for excavations. Erda has chemicals and meters to test the air, water, and land. And Celeste's gear is mostly radiation detection stuff. Of course, the only thing you brought fits in your shirt pocket. It's your Walkman-size portable computer.

Then you go over to help Olano on with his parachute. Since he's never jumped before, he has a special chute. "You didn't seem surprised by what happened before," you say to him as you buckle the harnesses.

"The Boranu jungle frightens and fascinates me — but it never surprises me," he says.

"Do you think the energy source was messing up our computers?" you ask.

"No, Orion," Olano says. "I think it was trying to kill us."

A yellow light flashes and a buzzer sounds. Jump time. Everyone lines up as the co-pilot opens the rear door of the jet. Green light — go! One by one the ACT members leap into the hurricane-force wind outside the plane. Celeste . . . Digger . . . you . . . Erda . . . Olano. And one by one the parachutes, with the red and purple ACT colors, open at 5,000 feet.

"My chute's not opening!" Olano suddenly shouts into his headset microphone.

You look up and see Olano falling like a rock.

CHAPTER
5

Erda is closest to Olano as the ACT crew falls through space. He makes a grab for Olano, but grabs only air.

"I missed him," Erda shouts into his headset.

"Olano!" you call. "Listen to me! Spread out! Lie flat — it'll slow your fall." But you can tell by the sound of his breathing in your headset that Olano is not aware of anything else in the universe except his fear. You watch him fall. Your hands are tensed to make a grab. But then you can see that he won't pass anywhere near you. "Digger, he's heading for you. Grab anything!" you shout.

"Forget it. I can't. The impact will tear our arms out or kill us both," Digger says.

"No!" Olano shouts, suddenly coming to

life. He spreads his arms and legs, slowing himself down in a pretty decent imitation of sky-diving. But Digger doesn't move as Olano passes by.

"Steady — steady," Celeste says. "You're coming toward me now — try to glide my way. I see you."

Celeste has something in her hand but you can't tell what. Then suddenly Olano grabs hold of her legs and the two of them fall like a bad trapeze act. When her arm comes up, you see the sun flash off the steel blade of a knife.

For a split second Celeste and Olano stare into each other's eyes, and then her arm swings quickly. The knife flashes again and Olano's chute bursts open. He is floating like a snowflake and laughing and crying like a madman.

You land and help one another fold up your chutes. Olano sits on the ground, staring at the earth and running his fingers through it.

"What happened up there?" you ask.

"It looked like his chute was fixed so it wouldn't open," Celeste says, looking grim.

"Do you recognize where we are? How far from the temple are we?" Digger asks, looking at the forest that completely surrounds the clearing you've landed in.

"Let him catch his breath," Celeste says.

"Thanks," Olano says. "Thanks to both of you," he says to you and Celeste. Celeste smiles.

"Well, we knew there wouldn't be a

marching band to greet you, so we had to do something special," Erda says with a laugh. "But seriously, are you feeling better?"

"Yeah, I'm feeling better," Olano says. "Let me see a map. Can you give me an exact location reading?"

"Sure," you say, wiping away the sweat that has suddenly started to drip from your forehead. You reach for your computer. But your hand shakes and the instant the computer hits the air, an alarm starts ringing.

But you don't need an alarm to tell you that you're in big trouble. You know what's going on. It's the one thing you feared most when you heard that this assignment involved contact with an unknown atmospheric force.

Suddenly, before you can speak, you're on your knees. How did you get there? Your head is so heavy that it topples you over like a cut tree and you're facedown in moist dirt. The others turn you over quickly.

"I've seen this before on digs — change of altitude and all that," Digger says. "Back off and give Orion some air."

"This doesn't look like hyperventilation to me," Celeste says. "Orion looks sick." She takes a quick measurement of the air. "Radiation level is above normal, but not approaching dangerous."

Erda, too, is measuring the air. "I've seen this before, too," he says. "But it's not dizziness — it's air pollution."

23

You try to talk, but you cannot make a sound. The nausea is overpowering; you wish you could turn your stomach inside out — or die. How can you tell them that something happened on your last ACT mission into outer space that left you weakened and vulnerable to strange and rare elements in the air? And if your voice doesn't come back, how can you warn them that the wrong treatment will kill you instantly?

"Nitrogen and carbon dioxide are giving me negative factors, but I'm also getting indications of materials I don't recognize," Erda says. "But they're in such small quantities that I'm going to ignore them. Hand me the medical kit."

Celeste tosses the kit to Erda, who snaps open the bag and takes out a syringe and several vials. You've got to stop him. Those small quantities of unrecognizable elements may not mean much to Erda, but they're life and death to you! If it's only a nitrogen imbalance or too much retrium in the air, then you'll probably snap out of this in a few minutes. But if it's the Devorim Force — don't think about it! Just do something!

"Orion, I'm going to give you an injection," Erda tells you. "You're going to feel like you're on a roller coaster for a couple of minutes, but then you'll be okay."

"No." You croak out the word. Your throat is as dry as burned toast, but you keep shaking your head no and inch your right hand toward your pocket.

"Look! Orion wants the computer," Olano says. He takes it out of your pocket and hands it to you.

Kneeling on the ground, you stare at Erda's air-quality instruments. Then you start entering the data into your computer.

"Retrium, 3.3." Your fingers shake as you type in the readings for the first element. Four more to go. "Hydrogen, 12.8; Delios, 66.3; Xenon, 71.7; Radon, 2.5." Now for the program you wrote to warn you if you are in real danger.

Type this program into your computer and run it. Enter the values for the five elements when asked. Lines 60, 270, and 390 should each be typed as one line on your computer.

If you can, save this program. You will need it again.

PROGRAM 2

```
10  REM ELEMENT ANALYSIS
20  DIM A(9)
30  C = 0
40  PRINT
50  DATA   "RETRIUM.","HYDROGEN"
60  DATA   "DELIOS..", "XENON...",
    "RADON..."
70  FOR I = 1 TO 5
```

```
 80  READ B$
 90  PRINT "WHAT IS VALUE FOR ";B$;
100  INPUT A(I)
110  NEXT I
120  RESTORE
130  PRINT
140  PRINT "RESULTS OF ANALYSIS"
150  PRINT "-------------------"
160  FOR I = 1 TO 5
170  READ B$
180  C = 13*ABS(SIN(A(I)))
190  PRINT B$;"   ";
200  FOR J = 1 TO C
210  PRINT "*";
220  NEXT J
230  IF C > 5 THEN GOSUB 340
240  PRINT
250  NEXT I
260  PRINT
270  PRINT "WANT TO SEE THE BOTTOM LINE
     (Y/N)";
280  INPUT Y$
290  IF Y$ = "Y" THEN 320
300  PRINT "OK. BUT YOU'LL WISH YOU HAD!"
310  END
320  GOSUB 370
330  END
340  N$ = B$
350  N1 = C * 1.3 + N1
360  RETURN
370  IF N1 < 15 THEN 450
```

```
380 PRINT
390 PRINT "DEVORIM FORCE AT LEVEL "
    ; INT(N1)
400 IF N1 < 23 THEN 430
410 PRINT "YOU ARE ABOUT TO DIE!"
420 GOTO 460
430 PRINT "YOU ARE IN GRAVE DANGER!"
440 GOTO 460
450 PRINT "YOU ARE SAFE—FOR NOW"
460 RETURN
```

IBM	Apple		Radio Shack		Commodore		TI	Atari
PC & PCjr	II+	IIe	TRS-80	Color	64	VIC-20	99/4A	400/800
✓	✓	✓	✓	✓	✓	✓		

This program will run on all the personal computers checked in the chart above. See the Reference Manual, page 118, for changes for TI and Atari.

Celeste stares at your monitor. "The Devorim Force — I've heard of it, of course," she says. "But I've never seen it affect anyone this way. Orion, is there anything we can do?"

"Yes," you croak. "Antidote — in there." You point to your gear and Celeste rummages through it until she finds a little green bottle of pills. She places one on the back of your tongue.

At the same time, Olano opens his shirt and removes a short necklace of small wooden and silver beads from his neck. At the center of the necklace is a polished silver disk. He slips the necklace over your head. Immediately your muscles relax and you feel fine again.

Once you're on your feet, you explain to Celeste and the others about the vulnerability you developed after space travel. "ACT's medics told me that this combination of elements is called the Devorim Force. Apparently I am very sensitive to it. That's why I wrote the program to analyze it and warn me."

"Will you be okay now?" Erda asks.

"I don't know," you say. "ACT Medical hasn't been able to figure out how to treat me. They could only come up with an experimental antidote and I'm not sure how it will work." And you silently add to yourself, *More exposure to the Devorim Force and it could be curtains.*

"If you can travel, we'd better get started," Celeste says. "My energy scanner says that a strong energy force lies somewhere north of here. So I vote to go north."

"Yes," Olano says. "My village is north of here. So I agree. But we need to be sheltered before nightfall," Olano says.

"Why?" you ask.

"Because it's a jungle out there, remember?" Olano says with a laugh.

"So, okay, guide. Lead on to the Boranu Holiday Inn," Erda says.

You and Olano take the lead. As you enter the forest and start walking north, you say to Olano, "You know, you didn't have to give me your necklace."

"Hey, speaking of that necklace," Digger calls out, "if you think I believe for one second that your necklace cured Orion and the pill didn't, you'd better think again."

"That's why I did not give the necklace to you," Olano tells Digger. Then he turns back to you and says, "Whatever happens to the rest of us will not happen to you. Do you believe that now, Orion?"

Unfortunately there isn't time for you to make up your mind or answer. Digger is calling to you — yelling at the top of his thin voice.

"Wait, you guys. Come back. It's Celeste! We're going to lose her!"

CHAPTER
6

You rush back 50 feet to a dense tree area where Celeste is suspended upside down from the thick limb of a tree. At first it looks like she is tangled up in a fat vine. But when you move a little closer, you see that there is an enormous snake wrapped around her.

"Shoot it! Shoot it fast!" shouts Erda.

"Don't!" Celeste says. The snake is wrapped so tightly that she can only speak in a breathy whisper. "It squeezes me harder every time anyone moves."

"Shoot it and you'll shoot her, too," Digger says, talking now in a softer voice.

"Got another necklace?" Erda asks Olano.

"One of these snakes, fully grown," Olano says, "can crush an elephant."

You reach into your pocket and you hear the tree rustle as the snake tightens its grip again. Celeste moans in agony. Carefully, quietly, you use your computer to zap a high-frequency signal at the snake. Instantly, the snake's head begins to twitch and jerk. It doesn't seem to know how to let go of Celeste. But finally it releases her, and you end the program. The snake slides away into the overgrown trees.

Celeste is okay except for a couple of cracked ribs and a bruised ego about not being better prepared.

"There's no way to prepare for the Boranu jungle," Olano says.

"But it wasn't the jungle that got me. It was something . . . human," Celeste says.

"What do you mean?" you ask.

"Somebody pushed me," she says. "I stopped to take a reading and someone pushed me from behind."

"As I told you," Olano says, "those who live here feel they have a great deal to protect. We are trespassers, don't forget."

"Don't forget about BRUTE, either," you say. "It could have been one of them who pushed Celeste toward that snake."

"I doubt it," Erda says. "BRUTE's not hanging around in the jungle waiting for us to show up. In fact, they've probably already made it to the temple."

"We're wasting precious daylight," Digger says. "If there is a temple around here, I'd like to see it."

"Digger's right," Olano says. "We can speculate later. We've got to move while it's still light."

The more you walk through the Boranu jungle the more of a personality it assumes — and it's not a pleasant personality. The jungle is moody. One moment you're walking through a clearing that's steamy and hot. The next moment you're in the middle of a thick brush area. Since no light can penetrate the enormous trees, it is chilly and damp.

You find yourself wondering why you ever came along on this mission — and then you immediately wonder if the Devorim Force has begun to affect your mind, too. It's not like you to be so down.

Maybe it's time for another green pill . . . but you wonder how long the supply will last.

Mission status: 10 hours down and 38 hours to go, according to Huntington's timetable. But in fact, you have no way of knowing whether BRUTE has already beaten you to the idol and used its power to take over the world. Maybe you're risking all of this for nothing! It sure is weird, getting along without instant information from television.

Your arms grow tired of chopping vegetation to clear a path. And you're sick of swatting away the large flying bugs that pester and prick at you.

"You must learn that living in the jungle is a compromise," Olano says, his voice in-

32

terrupting your thoughts. He is walking quickly and ignoring the bugs. "You will exhaust yourself fighting the bugs. Save your energy for larger opponents."

Hours later, when your legs are aching and your clothes are dripping and sticky with sweat, you reach another clearing. Olano pushes back a veil of vines and says, "Home, sweet home. This is where I was born. Not exactly San Francisco, is it?"

He laughs as you look at the cluster of huts around a community water well. Surrounding the area is farmland where the families still use oxen to plow and harvest. Then he leads you down into the village.

The people appear in their doorways and stare coldly until Olano steps forward. Then they begin to spill out of their houses and walk toward you. They seem curious and friendly — but slowly you realize you're being surrounded. Without saying a word, they separate Olano from you and move him toward the forest. He is trapped in a circle of bodies, which disappears into the mass of green trees. Soon the four of you are the only ones in sight.

An hour later Olano returns, but the villagers are still nowhere to be seen.

"What happened?" you and Celeste both ask.

"I don't exist. I am dead to them," Olano says. "Even if my life were in danger, they would not lift a finger to help me."

"Can't you explain why —" you start to say.

"I don't care about them," Olano interrupts. "It is only my father who worries me. He is very ill and they won't tell me where he is. They say he won't see me."

"You must have known it would be like this if you returned," Digger says. "Hasn't anyone ever left the village before?"

"No one," he says. "We are not uneducated people. But we do not believe in leaving the land we fought so hard to get. My leaving was an insult, a declaration that I do not love the land or these people."

"Pretty strict rules," Erda says.

"Strict rules come in handy living here," Olano says. "Now you four should rest for a while. If we are to reach the idol, I must find my father." He leaves, disappearing around a corner.

"How much time do we have left?" Digger asks you when he sees you looking at your watch.

"About 33 hours," you answer.

"That's what you told me when I asked you an hour ago," Digger says.

You, Celeste, and Erda all look at your watches and start shaking your wrists. The scene looks like a ridiculous comedy, except for the expressions on your faces.

"Nothing?" you ask Erda, who has actually held his digital watch up to his ear to see if it's ticking! *Some bunch of scientists,* you think to yourself.

But Erda shakes his head "no" and Celeste sets her jaw firmly.

"Well, look at it this way," she says. "If our watches have stopped, that must mean we're getting close to something with an incredible power to affect instrumentation. Maybe it's the Devorim Force, which would at least mean that we're close to the idol. By the way — how are you feeling, Orion? What are your biological instruments telling you?"

"I'm okay," you say. But unfortunately it's only because you've been hitting the green pills pretty regularly. The odds that they will last you another 30 hours are a million to one.

"All right. Start earning your scout badges. From now on we tell time by the sun," Digger says. "It looks like about noon to me. That gives us roughly 31 hours on Huntington's timetable."

"Look — forget that!" Celeste snaps. "BRUTE had a running head start on us. There's no time left in our schedule. When you're racing against a group of thoroughly power-crazed maniacs, 31 hours is like 31 minutes! I wish Olano would get back here!"

Just then a voice speaks at Celeste's ear, and she jumps a mile.

"We must leave now. I have learned of someone who might know where the temple is," is all Olano says.

Silently you and the others pick up your gear and follow him into the jungle once again. The path is narrow, but luckily it is one that has already been made.

The air in the jungle is wet and thick, but the tension is thicker. How long will it be before somebody snaps? Olano keeps an even faster pace now. You wonder whether it's because he's hurrying toward something or hurrying away.

Celeste's ribs are still hurting from her encounter with the snake, but it just makes her push harder. Occasionally she calls out that her radiation readings are getting higher.

But you don't need to be told that, because you already know that you are getting nearer and nearer to the Devorim Force. You need to stop and rest more frequently. Olano always stops for you and no one utters a word of complaint. But you know what's going through their minds, because it's the same thing that's going through your mind: Are you going to make it? Or are you going to be the reason BRUTE beats you to the temple and blows this continent to bits?

You decide to run your analysis program again. "Give me the readings, Erda," you say, trying not to sound too concerned.

"Sure, Ace," he says. "Retrium, 13.2; Hydrogen, 60.9; Delios, 6.8; Xenon, 45.5; Radon, 101.5."

If you were able to save Program 2, call it up now. If not, input it again; you'll find it on page 25. Run it and enter these readings for the five elements when the computer asks for them.

You power down immediately so that no one can see the bad news on the screen. "The Devorim Force is easing up," you lie through your teeth. Then you dampen a cloth, tie it around your forehead, and pick up your gear once more. "Let's not sit around here on my account," you say.

CHAPTER
7

"Hey, wait! I'm sinking! Come back!" Erda shouts. Suddenly, in less than 10 seconds the ACT crew is down to four-and-a-half members. By the time you've all turned around, Erda is up to his waist in quicksand.

"Don't fight it," Olano shouts.

"That's easy for you to say," Erda snaps.

"Get a move on," Digger says. "I've seen them go down faster than you can blink."

With one swing of a machete, Olano chops down a long, thick vine, and then he starts swinging it like a lariat to throw to Erda.

"Forget it," Digger says. "He can't catch it. His arms are stuck in the muck."

Erda isn't saying anything now. Only his head and neck are visible above the sticky goop. He's just looking at you with wide eyes.

"Half a million dollars worth of electronic equipment with us and we can't do anything to save a man's life?" Celeste demands bitterly.

Meanwhile, Olano has tied the vine around his waist. "When I tell you to pull, I don't want to see any halfhearted tries. We get one chance only!" Then he takes a long running leap into the quicksand and lands exactly in the spot where Erda *was* a second before. Olano thrashes about wildly, slowly being sucked under, himself. He twists and turns and you can't tell whether he's caught Erda or not.

Finally, Olano turns his head back to you and shouts, "Pull!!"

The three of you pull as hard as you can, but it's like pulling someone through cement. A couple of hard tugs later you see that Olano has Erda under the arms and around the chest. Erda is gasping for breath. One more pull and they're out!

Back on solid ground, Erda and Olano tear off their muddy clothes.

"That was quite a jump," you say to Olano.

"Purdue broad-jump team," Olano says, still trying to catch his breath. "I'm supposed to make All-America this year."

"You've got my vote," Erda says.

As the day warms up, the heat and humidity are exhausting everyone, but you have an extra problem. Your energy is draining noticeably. Erda and Celeste take some of your supplies so that your backpack is lighter to carry. But still, the farther you walk, the more you feel like most of your weight is in your feet.

That's the bad news. The good news is the weaker you get, the more you know that the temple must be near.

"You can rest here for a while," Olano says, "while I go into this village and talk to the man who is supposed to have seen the temple. If he sees all of you, he may ask an enormous price for the information."

Olano goes into the village and the rest of you have no trouble resting.

"Cheer up, gang," Erda says. "This is the easy part of the mission. Finding the temple and Professor Ballaster is going to be nothing compared to neutralizing that atomic statue."

"And taking it away from BRUTE — don't forget about them," you remind Erda.

"You keep saying that," Erda says. "I haven't forgotten about them. I've just temporarily chosen not to think about them. Hey, Celeste, you think you can turn this atomic light bulb off?"

"If I can't shut it down, I've got something in my pack that should destroy it," Celeste says.

"Wait a minute. You nuclear people are only happy when you've got a button to push," Digger says, waking out of a short but loud, snoring nap. "If this statue is an icon left here by an extraterrestrial civilization, you can't just blow it to smithereens. It's got to be studied in detail. I haven't come all this way just to see your fireworks show."

"You're out of line, Digger," Celeste says.

"Well, I'm telling you now: I'll do what I have to, to keep you from destroying the statue!" Digger says.

"Hey, Digger, I thought you were the one who said Ballaster had wind whistling between his ears," Erda says.

"Yes, but then again, this might be a once-in-a-lifetime discovery," Digger says. "You're a scientist. You should know that."

"Well, here comes the man who can tell us whether we're in business or not," Erda says, seeing Olano returning.

"Great news! I have a map and the temple is not far," Olano says. "I think we can make it in a couple of hours."

"Do you believe this man has actually seen the temple?" Digger asks skeptically.

"The man was an elder of the village," Olano explains, unfolding the map. "He is also about 7'2" and weighs 400 pounds."

"So what?" Digger says, taking the map out of Olano's hands. "That doesn't mean that he was telling the truth, does it?"

"But it does mean I'm going to be very careful about calling him a liar," Olano says. "Besides, it was my father who told me about this man. Now let's stop wasting time."

"I thought you said that your father would not see you," you say as you and Olano take the lead together again. "What changed his mind?"

"You," Olano says. "You see, I forced my way into the shack where he is staying. He is ill and bedridden, which didn't give him much choice about seeing me. He didn't say anything for what seemed like hours."

"What did he do all that time?" you ask.

"He looked at my clothes and my shoes and my hands. Then I gave him photos I brought of the university and my room and some of my friends. That's when he spoke. He asked me where my necklace was."

Your hand automatically reaches for your neck to feel the small wooden and silver beads of Olano's necklace that you now wear.

"He thought I had thrown it away. So I told him I had given it to one of the friends I had come with to be certain that at least one of us would escape the jungle," Olano says.

"Cut it out. We're all going to make it back home," you say.

"Then I told him why I had come back to the jungle. He said even if I survive the temple, I will bear its curse the rest of my life," Olano says with no particular emotion at all.

Could a father really carry through on a threat like that? You will know the answer to that question within the next 24 hours. But for now, it looks as if you are going to be very busy — exploring the ancient temple that has just come into view!

CHAPTER
8

For the first time since the mission began, Digger is smiling. The temple in front of you is an ancient structure and it's hard to believe that something so tall and massive was constructed without the help of a steam shovel.

"Well, first I've got to see how old this baby is," Digger says excitedly.

"Wait a minute. Something's missing. Where's the statue?" you ask.

"Probably around the other side," Digger says, opening up his equipment case. "Get it? We've approached the temple from the rear. Do I have to explain everything to you people?"

"I'm not getting very high radiation readings," Celeste says.

"Terrific. It's the wrong temple," you say, shaking your head. "Those dials should be spinning like a broken cuckoo clock."

"There's no reason to jump to conclusions," Digger says. "Knowing Ballaster, he got his descriptions mixed up and the idol is inside."

"Okay, Olano and I will check the other side of the temple," you say.

"Well, I'm going in," Digger announces. "This may be the only temple I see on this expedition, since some people's reliable sources aren't very reliable, if you ask me." Digger marches off, muttering to himself, "Mission? Wild goose chase is more like it."

"Wait, Digger," Erda says. "You'd better not go in alone. The place may not be safe."

They duck inside and Celeste catches up with you and Olano. "Tempers are getting short. What went wrong, Olano?" she asks.

"Two possibilities," Olano says. "The old man didn't completely understand my language or he deliberately sent us in the wrong direction. As I said, people around here are very protective about the temple."

"Digger seems to think there's a third possibility: Are *you* being protective about the temple, too?" she asks.

"No," Olano says.

Ptchewwwwing! Suddenly you hear gunshots! Three, then four. You run for the other side of the temple. Erda comes running toward you with a gun in his hand.

"BRUTE agents!" he shouts. "I lost them inside. They're getting out the back!"

The four of you race around back again. You stop and listen for a second. Something is racing away through the trees.

"There they go," Erda shouts. "Come on!"

"Forget it," Olano says. "We'll never catch them."

"We can try," Erda says.

"We can't leave Orion here in this condition," Olano says. The others turn around then and see that you've collapsed on the ground. Too much running for your weakening condition.

"Sure, you can leave me," you say, breathing heavily. "Besides, Digger's here."

"No, he's not," Erda says. "They got him."

"Well, if he's hurt, let's go," Celeste says.

"He's not hurt," Erda says, putting a hand out to stop Celeste. "He's dead."

"What? What happened?" you finally say when your brain starts feeding your mouth again.

"We got separated; he wouldn't wait for me. The BRUTE agents must have been waiting for us. Probably they just took one look at his ACT ID patch and closed in on him. They threw him into a hole, a pit in the temple. I heard him scream and came running with my gun firing at anything that moved. They got away. And when I yelled down the hole for

45

Digger all I got was a long, deep echo." After telling the story, Erda walks away and sits down under a tree.

The other three of you gravitate toward the temple and very carefully step in. It takes a second for your eyes to adjust to the dark. When they do, you see mostly crumbled columns and debris. In the center of the temple there is an enormous, deep pit.

The floor of the temple is dirt, not stone. In the earth near the pit, you see one of Digger's sharp picks.

"He said this might be the only temple he'd get to see on this mission," Celeste says, her voice a mixture of sadness and anger.

"How could this happen?" you say. "It's just not fair!"

"It seems that the people of your world have pretty strict rules, too," Olano says.

This is the part of the job you can't get used to. Veterans in the organization tell you that you will — but you don't believe them for a minute. But there's another truth you can't escape: The mission has to go on; the clock is still running.

"Well, there's nothing we can do for him now," Celeste says. "We have to move on." Turning to Olano, she asks, "Where should we go now?"

"I know the area to the south pretty well," Olano says. "And the temple's not there. So let's head north."

Heading in any direction just seems to take you deeper into the thickness of the jungle. Slowly the hours turn into long, silent miles. Erda is the quietest of all. He seems like a different person now — removed from the rest of the team.

Suddenly a loud noise pierces the monotony — a sound like something sliding or rolling down the hillside. Erda pivots toward the sound. His gun is drawn and cocked in a flash.

"Shoot me," a man's voice pleads. The man slowly stands up, wobbly and dizzy on weak legs.

Suddenly the man's face clicks into your memory. "It's Professor Ballaster!" you shout and start to run to him.

"Don't come near me," the professor says.

"We're here to help you, Professor," Celeste says, walking toward him with you.

"STOP!!" he screams. "I know who you are. If you want to help me, shoot me now!"

CHAPTER

9

Professor Ballaster is staggering and stumbling in circles on the narrow path in front of you. Maybe he's delirious with fever — maybe he's just gone nuts.

"I told them where it is," he says. "I had to. They tortured me. I never knew there were so many inhuman things they could do to a person. I told them. I had to."

"That's okay, Professor. We understand," Erda says. "But now you have to tell us where the temple is."

"I told them, but I didn't tell them why they shouldn't go in — because they'll never get out," the professor says.

"Did you actually take them to the temple?" Erda asks.

"No — I didn't have to. They were foolish enough to think that they could find it by themselves."

"Where is it?" Erda asks.

"Come on, wait a minute," Celeste says. "Let's do something to help him."

"Stay back — you can't help me," the professor says and laughs like an animal. "After they got the information, they injected me with a deadly virus — highly communicable, of course. Then they turned me loose, hoping I'd find my way to you. Now do you understand why I want you to shoot me?"

"Professor, look at me. It was I who told you to come to the Boranu jungle," Olano says.

The professor stares at him for a minute and finally smiles his recognition.

"Tell me where we can find it," Olano says again.

"Continue on this path, but to the east. You must cross the Yengo River at its widest point between two rocks that look like turtles. Eventually you will come to a wall of vines. It is not a wall; it is a door. Just beyond is the temple and the statue." The professor stops talking and suddenly stands rigidly, as though something were crawling up his body.

"Why shouldn't we go in?" you ask, hoping the answer will be about legends and spirits rather than something real.

But the professor cannot answer any more questions. He is no longer aware that you are even there as the virus attacks his brain. His face is horrible as he hits the ground and sighs his last breath.

"Can't we at least bury him?" you say, already knowing the answer.

"No — he's contaminated," Erda answers, backing away. Celeste nods in agreement, and you all pick up your gear for what seems like the hundredth time, and move on.

There is no time to waste. BRUTE has more than a head start. The only thing in your favor is the fading sun. If BRUTE hasn't reached the temple yet, they will probably camp during the night. You talk it over and decide to risk continuing on after dark — it's your only chance.

Nothing on this mission has been easy, and crossing the Yengo River at night is not going to change that perfect record. The river is white water — deep and wide and fast-flowing.

"We'd better wait till daylight to cross it," Olano says when you finally reach the river-bank. "If one of us breaks away and heads downstream, we'll never find each other."

But the ACT team disagrees. It's now or never. BRUTE won't wait. So Celeste and Olano tie buddy ropes around their waists and you and Erda do the same. Then you all walk into the river. It's difficult just to stand in the moving water, but you walk out as far as you can before plunging in to swim. It's not just swimming. It's fighting for your life with every ounce of strength in your body. Forget about graceful, controlled strokes. You swing your arms as hard as you can and hope that you are carried forward a little.

When you look over at Erda, he tries to give you a smile. "ACT team? I'm going to be ready for the Olympic team after this mission," he shouts.

It's just the right thing to say to pick up your spirits and get you to move your aching arms one more time and then another and then another.

Then, suddenly, your feet touch bottom. You've made it. You and Erda stand up and stumble, exhausted, to the shore. But you can't rest yet. You have to build a fire to keep from getting chilled and to signal your location to Olano and Celeste.

They join you in a few minutes and fall down in front of the fire, too tired to untie the rope around their waists.

"Let's keep going," Celeste says the minute she's dry. "We must be close to the temple now and the longer we stay here, the worse Orion is going to get."

But Olano says no. "It took Ballaster years to find the temple. We'd never find it in the dark. We'll camp here for the three remaining hours of night, and then make a fresh start at dawn."

As you eat some food and recover, Olano begins to talk about the temple you are very near — the temple he has heard about and feared all of his life.

"For generations tribes fought over possession of the temple. Some thought it was sacred. Others just wanted it so that no one else could have it. I had a great-uncle who said that he once saw the great statue," Olano says.

"When?" you ask immediately.

"Many years ago. At that time, my great-uncle was a warrior for Chief Teliru. Teliru was what you could call an equal-opportunity tyrant. He would steal from everyone — the poor as well as the rich. And because of the size of his army, he could go anywhere and take anything he wanted in the jungle. It was even said that once it didn't rain for five years because the sky was afraid of Teliru."

Olano's words, combined with the strange jungle noises, give you the feeling that just beyond the flame of your campfire is the sacred temple and a wild, unfamiliar life.

"Teliru eventually ran out of tribes to conquer and villages to burn. The only thing left unchallenged was the temple. And Teliru was not a man to let anything go unchallenged. But he was not a fool, either. So, according to my great-uncle, Teliru didn't tell his army just exactly where they were going." Olano stops for a second and smiles. "Listen," he says. "Drums."

You both listen for a minute — you with curiosity and Olano with deliberate attention. "Someone knows we are here and is passing the word along," he says. "They say that the man with the walking stick is a traitor and is no longer their friend. And they are happy he is dead."

"That must be Ballaster," Celeste says. Olano nods.

"What about your great-uncle?" you ask. "What happened when he went into the temple? Obviously, if he told you the story, it didn't kill him."

"It took Teliru two years, but finally he found the temple. He proclaimed it as his own and to prove that he was fearless and invincible, he attacked the statue. A secret entrance opened up. And Teliru and his army marched into the interior of the temple."

"And then what?" you ask impatiently.

"Once inside, my great-uncle said he had a vision. It was a vision of himself — a plain and simple farmer by a clear, blue stream. So my great-uncle decided to follow his vision and not his general and he ran out of the temple as fast as he could."

"And Teliru?" Erda asks.

"He and all of his men were never seen again — although, according to my great-uncle, they were heard. He heard them screaming inside the temple, screaming in unimaginable torture. Then he heard nothing," Olano says.

"Legend or fact?" Erda asks.

"My great-aunt, who lived many years longer than my great-uncle, told me something. She said that the secret of her long life was never believing anything my great-uncle said. So I don't know if any of it is true,'' Olano says with a smile.

"I guess we'll soon find out," you say.

You walk over to the fire and throw on some wood. The wood supply is getting low. So you decide to scout the perimeter of the camp for some more usable wood. The sounds in the forest are busy. Animals skitter through the brush, calling to one another, challenging one another — and challenging you, too. Suddenly you recognize one of the sounds in the brush — footsteps. They are quiet and light, but they are unmistakable.

"Who's there?" you call out, flashing your light in the direction of the sound. But then the sound comes from a different side. "Who is it?" you say again calmly. You back up toward the camp, toward the blazing fire. The sounds are still. Then there's a loud snap behind you and you jump into the air. You wheel around poised to fight . . . but it was only a twig in the fire. You can't help it — you've got to laugh at yourself. So you throw a little more wood on the fire and turn on the microlink communicator the team brought on this mission.

As you turn the frequency control you hear a coded message being sent out. Obviously the location of the transmitter is very near you. Perhaps it's BRUTE sending a message! Quickly you reach for the cable to interface the radio with a decoder program in your portable computer.

Whip!! Your arms sting for a second and then you can't feel them. *Whip!!* The sting hits your legs and then you can't feel them, either. You are encircled by some kind of cord or vine. There's a hand over your mouth so you cannot call out. And other arms are dragging you away from the camp. You twist to see your attackers, but they pull a cloth bag over your head and tie it around your neck. There is nothing you can do. You are their prisoner!

CHAPTER

10

With your arms and legs tied tightly, and your head covered with a cloth bag, you are carried swiftly on the shoulders of your abductors. When you arrive at your unseen destination, you are untied and thrown into some sort of room with a dirt floor. Your hands immediately rip at the ties on the bag, but removing it doesn't throw much light on your predicament.

The room you're trapped in is as dark as the bag you were enclosed in. You wait for your eyes to adjust to the darkness. But you soon realize that even if you wait a hundred years, you still won't be able to see your hand in front of your face. And you don't have a hundred years — you've got less than 24 hours to wrap this mission up.

So you walk straight ahead. Twenty paces later you bump into a wall. You turn and walk back in the other direction. Twenty-five paces later you hit another wall. No tables, chairs, or beds — just walls. You walk around the edge of the room, feeling the walls with your hands. But you don't find what you're looking for. There are no windows and no door latch on the inside. *Whoever these guys are,* you think, *they don't mess around.* But then neither do you. You reach to trigger the emergency homing device in the heel of your boot. But you aren't wearing boots now. That's strange. You thought sensation was back in your arms and legs, but it must not be completely. Those stings in your arms and legs must have been darts — tranquilizer darts, not poisonous ones.

Okay, it makes sense, you think to yourself, rubbing your feet. If they are BRUTE agents, they'd know about the homing device in the boot. But why hold you captive? Why not just get rid of you right away?

You'll find out all the answers you need tomorrow. But first things first: You've got to get through the night, so you've got to stop thinking about BRUTE and their appreciation for the more painful things in life — like torture. What should you do? Should you wonder what your family is doing right now? No — definitely not! You've got to stir up a little action. Why should you wait until *they're* ready to talk?

You're back on your feet quickly and you

start pounding on the walls. Suddenly you hear a door open on the other side of the room. It's not open long enough for your eyes to see anything, but you can hear that it's open long enough for your captors to throw something into the room.

"What's going on around here?" you shout. "Don't you guys ever pay your electricity bill? Just who are you, anyway?"

This time you get a reply. It comes from somewhere inside the room with you. But it's not the kind of reply you were hoping for. It's the heavy sigh and then the low, rumbling growl of some kind of animal.

You back away as far from it as you can and scrunch down on the floor. That's how you spend the rest of the night — in horrible, expectant silence.

Later — no way to tell how much later . . . hours? minutes? days? — the door opens and sunlight hits you like an ocean wave, knocking you back, blinking and squinting. You jerk involuntarily, but then you remember that you're not alone in your sealed cell. You squint around the room for the animal that guarded you all night. There, against the wall, is an enormous, ancient, fat dog. It looks at you, yawning, trying to stay awake. But the effort is a failure and it puts its heavy head back down on the ground. Still you walk past it cautiously, even though its tail wags a little as you leave the cell.

Outside, the sunlight and fresh air feel and smell good. Your new surroundings don't look that promising, however. There are two guards with long machetes posted on either side of the door as you walk out of the shack. They move as you move, blocking your path. They are silent, but it's a case of glares speaking louder than words.

You're in a village, a large, but poor village; it's definitely not the sort of place BRUTE agents would hang out in. So you decide you've been kidnapped by a jungle tribe and not by BRUTE. The thought gives you a strange but uncalled for feeling of relief. Then a thin rope is thrown around your neck and you are led like a dog into a small straw shack. There is a large crowd inside the shack and their faces are no more friendly than those of the people outside. At the center of the room sits a tall man in a large chair that goes beyond "chair" and enters the category of "throne." He points, and someone gives you a carved gourd filled with water. *Thank goodness for small favors*, you think.

You and the tall man stare at each other. Now that they've had their fun, it looks like you'll get some straight answers. But his face is momentarily confused. Apparently he is not used to people staring at him directly. Finally he breaks the silence, but when he begins to speak, you can't understand a word of his language. He talks for a while, gesturing broadly with enormous hands. At one point the room erupts in laughter when the man in the chair laughs.

Finally, you can't take it anymore and you interrupt. "Guys," you say, "I think what we have here is a failure to communicate. What are we going to do about it?"

The answer comes quickly. The thin rope is thrown at your head again. But this time, your reaction is swift. You sidestep the rope, catch it, and pull it with a jerk. That sends the man who threw the rope stumbling off-balance into the middle of the room.

"Who's next?" you shout, moving your arms as though you really had attended all of the ACT seminars on martial arts. Somehow, it didn't seem like a necessary skill for a hacker — until now.

The crowd roars with laughter, but then everyone becomes silent and turns toward the man in the chair. He is holding your portable computer in his hand. He pokes it, he squeezes it, he turns it; finally he drops it in frustration and steps on it.

"Programming can be tough to learn, but don't let it get you down," you say. And since no one else is laughing at your jokes, you laugh yourself. But that's a mistake, because the man in the chair thinks you are laughing at *him*! The crowd starts to close in, but before it does, you know what you have to do — even if you die trying. You make a dive for your computer on the floor. You scramble on your hands and knees, and as soon as you've got it in your hands, you do two things: set off the silent homing signal; and run a test program that uses as many beeps and tones as possible. It gets their attention, but it doesn't make them any less angry at you.

You've got to do something to break through the language barrier and you've got to do it at a speed that will break through the sound barrier. All at once you realize the one thing you have in common with the people of this village. It's right there on the back of the throne — the eye! The mysterious eye of the idol of Professor Ballaster's temple! You know the idol means something to them, but you won't know what — until after they see the program you're thinking up.

Type this program into your computer and run it. Note: Put six spaces between the quotes in line 80.

PROGRAM 3

```
10  REM THE IDOL'S EYE
20  DIM P(5)
30  HOME
40  DATA 0,4,5,6,6,5
50  FOR I = 0 TO 5
60  READ P(I)
70  NEXT I
80  O$ = "      "
```

```
 90  B$ = "@@@@@@"
100  C$ = "******"
110  FOR I = 1 TO 3
120  FOR J = 1 TO 12
130  V = J
140  IF I <> 3 THEN 160
150  V = 13 - V
160  S$ = O$
170  G$ = C$
180  IF I <> 2 THEN 210
190  S$ = B$
200  G$ = B$
210  L = 20 - 2 * ABS(6 - V)
220  IF V > 6 THEN L = L + 2
230  H = 7 - V
240  IF V <= 6 THEN 260
250  H = V - 6
260  HTAB (H): VTAB (V)
270  PRINT "**";
280  N = P(6 - H)
290  G = L - 2 * N - 4
300  IF N = 0 THEN 320
310  PRINT MID$(S$,1,N);
320  IF G <= 0 THEN 350
330  PRINT MID$(G$,1,G);
340  IF N = 0 THEN 360
350  PRINT MID$(S$,1,N);
360  PRINT "**"
370  NEXT J
380  FOR W = 1 TO 1000: NEXT W
390  FOR W = 1 TO 500
400  NEXT W
```

```
410 NEXT I
420 VTAB 20: END
```

IBM	Apple		Radio Shack		Commodore		TI	Atari
PC & PCjr	II+	IIe	TRS-80	Color	64	VIC-20	99/4A	400/800
	✓	✓						

This program will run on the Apple II and the Apple IIe as is. See the Reference Manual, page 120, for changes for the IBM, Radio Shack, Commodore, TI, and Atari.

The man on the throne is out of his chair and standing beside you in a split second! Now that he is standing up, you can see that he's enormous — and terrifying! And he's coming straight for you!

CHAPTER
11

The huge man looks from the computer to you and to the blinking eye on the computer again. Then he takes your right arm, stretches it to its full length, and then encloses it in his out-stretched right arm.

A tribal handshake? Now we're getting somewhere!

Then he escorts you to a different shack, another one guarded by men with machetes. But there's a twist. The two guards by the door are wearing cloth bags over their heads, probably cloth bags just like the one thrown over your head when you were kidnapped. Is this a joke? From a distance the tall man throws a small piece of cloth at the doorway. Before it touches the ground, the two guards strike, slicing the cloth to bits with their razor-sharp knives.

Guards who attack by sound, not sight.

Whatever is in that shack must be worth a bundle to these people. The tall man announces himself to the guards and they let you enter. Two other men come in, too.

The inside is stunning. The tall man goes right to a golden headdress, polished sun-bright, and places it on his head. In the center of the headdress is another replica of the idol's eye. The chief — it's obvious that's what he is — points to the eye and to your computer and extends his right arm again. You do the same, but your mind is busy taking in everything in the room. Everything is solid gold: small statues, candlesticks, torch handles, and several objects you've never seen before and can't imagine what they're used for.

Then the chief releases the other men from the room. When they are gone he lifts the protective covering off a solid gold scale model of what must be their sacred temple, the temple Professor Ballaster and so many thousands of others gave their lives for. It is just like the professor's drawing, except there are no vines covering it. And it is even more breathtaking in miniature. Although the model is only one foot high, you can tell that the temple is a tall building. There are thin, graceful columns and a beautiful arch carved with strange figures like the statue. The statue in the model is solid gold with a small diamond for the eye. Even this small, the eye is absolutely hypnotizing.

The chief then sweeps his arm in a wide circle. You get it — he means that the temple and all the surrounding territory belongs to him and to his people. Then he falls down on one knee and stretches out his right arm toward the model temple. He looks to you to see if you understand the gesture. You nod and get down on your knees to examine the model. You can't find an entrance, so you walk two fingers toward the temple, gesturing how to get in. The chief bats you away from the model with a quick sweep of his arm. He is saying that it should not be entered. And he writhes and weeps in a pantomime to show you what will happen if you enter.

Again you indicate to the chief that you want to know where the entrance is. But something suddenly catches the chief's eye. He walks over to you for a closer look. It's Olano's necklace. The chief examines it, smiling for the first time and shaking you playfully by the shoulders. You don't know what the necklace means to him. But his playful shaking practically jarred two fillings loose! Then the chief gives in. He again goes to one knee and stretches his right arm to the temple. Then he removes the roof of the model and shows you the inside.

Amazing! Wait till Digger gets a look at this! But then you remember — Digger's not going to see the temple. Ever.

There is a commotion outside, and you

realize that the rest of the ACT team has followed the homing device signal straight to you. Erda, Celeste, and Olano are calling for you at the tops of their voices. Quickly the chief demonstrates to you one more crucial piece of information. It is a route to the temple — a shorter way than the one Ballaster told you about. Then you and the chief step out of the shack. His golden headdress blazes in the sun.

"Hi, guys," you say. "What's up?"

"We were halfway to the temple when we finally started getting your homing signal," Celeste says. "We'd given you up for permanently lost."

"No, I wasn't lost. As a matter of fact, you might say I was found — they found me invading their land and decided to take me home. By the way, meet the chief," you say. "He owns the temple."

Olano immediately begins to ask the chief questions and the chief listens with patience while Olano tries out a number of languages. But in the end, he grasps your right hand again and disappears silently back into the shack. Then one of the chief's aides whispers something into Olano's ear.

"He said the chief has said all he's going to say on the subject," Olano says.

"Thanks for nothing," Erda says.

"Don't worry," you tell them. "The chief told me a shortcut to the temple and how to get in. I've got it all in my computer."

"How in the world did you talk to him??" Olano asks in disbelief.

"Hey, you've just got to speak their language, that's all," you say.

That could be your last joke for a while, because the shortcut to the temple is a treacherous one — over a sheer mountain. And the level of the Devorim Force will be much higher when you get there. And you've still got to deal with BRUTE before this mission is over.

And one more thing. You just took the last green pill from your bottle.

You promise yourself that from now on, you'll be very, very careful about every move you make. And you also decide that you won't mention your physical condition to anyone in the group again.

CHAPTER
12

"This is not what I call a shortcut," Erda says. He is the leader on the way up the mountain, having done some mountain climbing before. He sits on a small ledge, pulling the rope that helps you up.

"At the next ledge, there is a path cut out of the mountain," you say. "That's the shortcut."

"Because it cuts your life short by about 30 years to reach it — right?" he says.

Behind you, Celeste and Olano are making their slow way up. You slump on the ledge, trying to rest, trying to conserve your energy. Your computer has signaled another Devorim Force alarm.

"You've got the layout of the whole temple on your computer?" Erda asks, pulling Celeste up to join you. Three up and one more to go.

"Yes," you say and fish through your backpack for the computer just to make sure you've still got it. It's a long way back down to pick up something you dropped.

"Can I see it?" Erda asks, taking the computer from your hand. But he trips over a tie line, stumbles, and flies forward off the ledge. Celeste screams and you all freeze for one horrible instant, waiting to see if the tie-line will hold or break. Erda bounces like a yo-yo, but the line holds. He waves to you from 100 feet below as he dangles against the mountainside.

When the three of you — Olano, Celeste, and you — reel Erda back up to the ledge, he climbs up saying, "That was pretty dumb."

"We've lost time," Olano says.

"Worse than that — we've lost the computer. I dropped it," Erda says.

Everyone is too shocked to react as they wait for Erda to say this is another one of his jokes.

"Hey! Here it is!" you shout. "I must have pulled out my transistor radio by mistake — the Devorim Force must really be getting to me."

Erda gives you a big smile and a sigh. "You mean I only have to feel like half an idiot instead of a total idiot? That's a relief."

"Don't worry, Erda. You'll always be a total idiot to me," Celeste says with a laugh.

After that, the climb to the second ledge takes another hour, but the passageway to the shortcut is there exactly as the tribal chief promised. Caves and meandering tunnels have been carved through the mountain. They are filled with strange writings scratched and painted on the walls, and bats that seem to be your escort on this final leg of your journey. There are also a few giant spiders you consider addressing as "Sir." The four of you rush past them all, hoping the tunnel will open onto daylight around the next turn. The damp heat is making it tough for everyone to breathe, but it's even harder on you.

When the bats break away from you and turn back, Olano shouts as he runs, "We must be getting near!"

He's right! Sunlight so bright it slows you down bursts from the opening of the tunnel. But the vision outside the tunnel is unbelievable. The approach to this side of the temple is nothing like Professor Ballaster's old drawing. It isn't decaying and it isn't hidden by dense and twisted vines. The temple stands in the middle of a small green valley of flowers and fruit trees. And it glistens and sparkles in the sun from the gilding that seems to cover everything. The columns of the temple seem too slender and graceful to be able to support the golden archway with its strange carved figures. However, everything about this place defies your expectations.

"Why didn't Ballaster tell us?" Erda asks. "Why didn't he say that it was this beautiful?"

"Because he knew that the power of the statue isn't beautiful at all," Olano says.

"He must have made that drawing before he ever actually found the temple," you mutter to yourself. "If people knew, they'd start World War III over this place. I wish Digger could see it."

You have wandered away from the others and are now standing in front of the idol — it's 20 feet high, and like the chief's scale model, the idol is solid gold. But it's not at all the ominous image it was in Ballaster's drawing. Instead it fills you with a peaceful feeling — but it also makes you very sick. The statue is definitely the source of the strange element making you so ill.

"Look at the eye," you say to Celeste. "What is it made of?"

"Something out of this world," she says. "But I'm not getting readings off the statue anywhere near the strength the professor talked about."

"There's more to this temple than just this statue — much more," you say.

"How do you know?" Erda asks.

"Because the chief wouldn't tell me what was inside no matter how I asked him. He only said not to go in," you answer. "So — ready to go in?"

"Not yet," Erda says, putting a fresh clip of ammunition into his rifle. "Now I'm ready. How do we get in? Where's the secret entrance?"

"Watch this," you say. Then you kneel before the statue on one knee and stretch out your right arm toward it, the way the chief had shown you. With a great grinding noise, a door in the pedestal of the statue opens slowly. "Everyone looks for an entrance on the temple, but it's in the statue," you say. You look behind you. Celeste and Erda are following, but Olano is still standing transfixed by the sight of the temple. "You don't have to come in if you don't want to," you say. "Leading us here was your job — taking care of BRUTE is ours."

"I have heard about this temple, dreamed about it all my life and never in my wildest dreams believed it could be this beautiful. It is a shame you now have to destroy it," Olano says.

"We're not going to destroy it. We're going to save it," you say.

He takes one more look at the temple and then follows you through the door in the statue. It leads down some stone steps into a chamber underground.

"Look at the radiation readings I'm getting!" Celeste says. "What on earth is inside this place?"

"We won't know unless we can get

through the maze," you say, peering down into the darkness beyond the doorway.

"The maze?" Celeste says. "We don't have time for any guessing games."

"We don't have much choice," you say. "The chief showed me that the basement of this place is laid out like a maze. Whatever the secret of the temple is, it's a well-kept secret. It's smack in the middle of all of these passageways."

"Okay, and did he also tell you which way to go?" Celeste asks.

"Not in so many words. He kept pointing me in one direction and another. But I did find out that there are four main passageways to the maze. Each of the passageways begins at an arch that has a set of numbers on it. The numbers are a kind of code having to do with direction and distances, I think. I'm hoping my computer might be able to help us pick the right path."

Suddenly you hear a long, horrible scream from deep inside the temple.

"What was that?" Celeste asks.

"Well, I'll tell you this," Erda says. "It wasn't my stomach growling for lunch."

CHAPTER 13

You make your careful way down to the lower level. There, just as you imagined, is a cavern with four arches — each marking the beginning of another path. The numbers are clear now:

PATH 1: 16 25 30 27 12 17 10 7 4
PATH 2: 44 29 42 31 8 21 6 15 11
PATH 3: 16 25 22 35 8 26 7 14 23
PATH 4: 24 33 14 27 4 17 22 17 8

The chief told you that the "Good Path" makes a circle. Somehow, hidden in these numbers is a pattern that will take you to safety.

Then you see something else. There is a large, gold, four-pointed star on a wall near the entrance. Each point has an ornate number engraved on it.

"Is it a clock?" Celeste asks. "There's a zero where twelve o'clock should be." She shines her flashlight and keeps reading the numbers. "There's a two at three o'clock, a one at six o'clock. And there's a three at nine o'clock."

"No, I don't think it's a clock," you say, practically shouting in excitement. "I think it's a compass! If those numbers stand for east, west, north, and south, I just might have the key to the number code on the arches!"

By the light of Celeste's flashlight, you are programming your computer. Only one set of these numbers represents a round trip. If you get the system, you should be able to simulate the route and find the right path!

There's no need to be reminded that minutes and not hours remain of your 48-hour deadline. There's no need to be reminded that around any of those twists and turns could stand BRUTE agents waiting for you with outstretched arms — the kind of arms that shoot rounds of bullets. Even if you hold your breath, you can hear the fear in the loud, sharp breathing of your companions. It's always like this when a mission comes down to final actions — the crucial actions. Everything else has led up to this.

Type this program into your computer and run it. Lines 250 and 320 should each be typed as one line on your computer. Then choose one path to try. Type in the numbers that are inscribed over the arch leading to that path. Hit

RETURN after each number you type in. Listing the program and studying it may give you a clue as to which to choose.

PROGRAM 4

```
 10 REM *** MAZE ***
 20 DIM P(4), Z(4), C$(4), A1(9)
 30 DATA "N", "S", "E", "W"
 40 READ C$ (0), C$(1), C$(2), C$(3)
 50 PRINT "WHICH PATH ";
 60 INPUT J
 70 Z(J) = 0
 80 PRINT "ENTER 9 NUMBERS:"
 90 FOR I = 0 TO 3
100 P(I) = 0
110 NEXT I
120 FOR I = 1 TO 9
130 PRINT I; "->";
140 INPUT A1(I)
150 NEXT I
160 PRINT
170 PRINT "<PATH";J;">";
180 FOR I = 1 TO 9
190 A = A1(I)
200 B = INT(A / 4)
210 X = A - B * 4
220 P(X) = P(X) + B
230 PRINT B;C$(X);" ";
240 NEXT I
250 IF ABS((P(0) = P(1)) + (P(2) = P(3))) < 2
    THEN 270
```

77

```
260 Z(J) = 1
270 PRINT
280 PRINT
290 PRINT " ................................................"
300 I = J
310 IF Z(I) = 0 THEN 340
320 PRINT "PATH";I;" LEADS TO THE IDOL'S
    SECRET"
330 GOTO 350
340 PRINT "YOU WILL ** DIE ** ON PATH ";I
350 PRINT
360 PRINT "TRY ANOTHER PATH (Y/N)";
370 INPUT Q$
380 IF Q$ <> "Y" THEN 400
390 GOTO 50
400 END
```

IBM	Apple		Radio Shack		Commodore		TI	Atari
PC & PCjr	II+	IIe	TRS-80	Color	64	VIC-20	99/4A	400/800
✓	✓	✓	✓	✓	✓	✓	✓	

This program will run on all the personal computers checked in the chart above. See the Reference Manual, page 123, for changes for Atari.

"I know it's a computer," Olano says,

while everyone looks over your shoulder at the paths your computer has chosen, "but are you positive that it's right? I'm not used to entrusting my life to a machine."

"A computer is only as good as the person programming it," you say, shaking from the effects of the Devorim Force.

Olano looks at you and smiles. "Then I am content with my destiny," he says.

And so you set out to snake your way through the maze.

The four of you turn left, walk, then turn right, walk, and turn again. At every turn you shine your flashlights to try to see for sure if it is the right path. Some of the walls seem to glow red without giving off any heat or light.

All of a sudden, Erda begins to giggle, but he shuts it off, biting his lower lip. "Sorry," he says. "Nervous."

Loose dirt scratches under your feet on the stone floor and echoes as you walk. Suddenly in the middle of the next corridor, Olano grabs your arm roughly and pulls you back with a jerk. The light of his flashlight shines ahead to the space where you almost stepped. It is a huge gap in the floor — a place where the floor just stops. Then there's a six-foot drop . . . then three feet later the hallway continues as it was. He drops a stone down into the pit and it hits bottom quickly.

"Just a small pit — not enough to kill you, only enough to break your leg in the dark," he says. "We'll have to climb down to get across — one at a time. The floor could be triggered by weight."

One by one you crawl down one side of the small pit and climb up the other side. Your movements are slow and cautious, waiting to respond to instant catastrophe. When all of you get to the other side, you see that the floor drops off again into a somewhat deeper pit. This time you lower one another down one side and help pull one another up the other.

At the top of the second pit, you sigh with relief. But it's the wrong thing to do, because one step forward you suddenly feel yourself falling straight down. The stone floor has collapsed under you, starting an avalanche of dirt. You've been tricked. Those first two holes weren't the booby-traps — this one is!

You fall fast, the dirt covering over you in a ready-made grave. The wet earth presses against your face and for the first time you feel certain you're not going to make it through this mission. In fact, it's a tremendous relief to finally stop struggling for a minute. You feel yourself give in to it. *Just let go*, you say to yourself. . . . It feels so peaceful here, with the cool dirt against your mouth, filling your nostrils, lightly holding your eyelids closed.

ZRRRRRRRK! WARNING! FATAL ERROR! GET UP, ORION, AND GET OUT OF THERE!

Well, at least the old survival instincts still

kick in when they're supposed to. In four seconds flat you're pushing up, trying to stand against the weight above your head. For one split-second eternity, you were enjoying this hideous living grave, but now you're struggling against it with all the energy you have left. But hard as you try, you can't move.

Finally the nauseating sensation of being buried alive gives you an extra terrified jolt and you start flailing in all directions. It works — and you realize you were upside down in the pit. You were pushing the wrong way to get out. Now you're right side up and free.

You look for the others. Celeste is within arm's reach, Olano has pulled himself up out of the dirt, and Erda is clinging to the other side. A couple minutes later the ACT crew is ready to continue its way through the maze of the temple.

''Shine your light over here. There's something drawn on the wall,'' Celeste says.

You gather around to see a drawing of a man standing on another man's shoulders.

''Extraterrestrial graffiti?'' Erda asks.

It's as good an explanation as any and it gives each of you something to think about as you walk slowly down the dark paths.

Whoosh! Something sweeps past your head. *Whoosh!* It flies back the other way. And then it's back again.

More bats, you think to yourself — but that's before something shiny catches a little light from your flashlight — and before Olano screams out in pain. Everyone aims beams at the ceiling and quickly ducks down. Daggers, with points at both ends, are suspended from the ceiling on ropes and swing back and forth like deadly pendulums.

"I'm cut on the shoulder," Olano says. But luckily he's not seriously hurt.

"You lucked out," Erda says. "The daggers on the longer ropes would have struck straight at your heart."

"Crawl for it and keep close to the ground," Celeste says. But the farther you crawl, the lower the daggers hang.

"I can't crawl any farther — one just nipped my back," Erda says.

Suddenly Olano jumps to his feet, his machete in his hands flashing in one direction and then the other.

"Get down!" you shout to him.

As the daggers swing by, Olano's blade slices the ropes that tie them and they clink to the ground in pairs.

You're on your feet in a flash and ready to continue when Celeste stops you again. She spots a second drawing on the wall. This one is of a man reaching for a drape that covers the golden statue's hypnotic eye.

"It's a message of some kind," you say. "But what do these signs mean?"

"Don't look at the statue's eye?" Celeste asks.

"And what did that first sign mean?"

"No Piggyback Zone," Erda says with a big laugh.

"Shh," Celeste says. "BRUTE could be anywhere."

You keep walking, following the path your computer has mapped out for you. Then Erda gets the giggles again.

"Shhh!" Celeste says. "What's the matter with you?"

"Sorry, I just can't keep it in any longer. This is going to be too much fun," Erda says.

"What is?" you ask.

"Killing you," he answers, aiming his rifle at you.

CHAPTER 14

"Well, should I just kill you and get it over with, or should I explain what's going on and drag out the suspense?" Erda asks with a smile.

"You're calling the shots," you say.

He laughs. "That's a pretty good one."

"What do you want, Erda? Is it the gold?" Celeste asks.

"Call me Jack. I'm sick to death of your stupid code names. My name's Jack Assante. And, no, it's not the gold. What does BRUTE want with gold? It's the statue and the secret of its power — that's what we want," he says. "We want it so bad we even considered the possibility that we'd need your help getting it. Thanks for opening the door, kid. I'm sure my colleagues have joined me by now."

"And now you don't need us anymore," Celeste says.

"I think you're beginning to catch on," Jack says.

"A double agent. . . . How does it feel to be a lowlife and work both sides of the fence?" Celeste suddenly snaps.

"He's not a double agent," you say. "He's just a killer."

"What's that supposed to mean?" Jack asks nastily.

"It means you killed the real Erda," you reply.

"It seemed like the thing to do at the time," he says.

"And he killed Digger, too," you tell your companions. "There were no other BRUTE agents in that other temple."

"I get impatient sometimes," Jack says.

"The truth is, I've suspected you for a while," you say, "ever since you swam the Yengo River with me. I remembered then that the computer profile I read to you on the plane said that Erda never learned to swim. When you asked to see my computer, I knew."

"Not bad, kid," he tells you.

"That's why I deliberately handed you my radio instead of my computer on the mountain. And that's why I also went to a lot of trouble to fix your rifle when you set it down for a while," you say.

Jack doesn't smile; he doesn't say anything. He also doesn't believe you. So he squeezes the trigger hard. Nothing happens. He throws the rifle down in disgust. "Hey, you guys! This is Jack. Where are you?"

"Hold on a minute. We've got you on the heat sensor. We're on our way," a voice says over an intercom in Jack's pocket.

"So are we," you say, deciding not to wait to meet Jack's friends. Celeste smiles at you and says, "Nice work, Orion." And the three of you run the other way, taking some different turns along the way. When you stop, you're sure you've lost Jack and the other BRUTE agents . . . but then you realize you've also lost the way out of the temple. You wander for a while until you come again to the daggers lying on the floor. You've been wandering in circles and you're right back where you started from.

"Now what?" Celeste asks. "You know we can't stay down here forever soaking up this strange energy."

Of course, no one knows that better than you.

"Well, we can't go this way," Olano says, pointing in one direction.

"Why not?" you ask.

He takes a pen from his pocket and throws it on the ground in front of him. With a crash a steel-spike wall drops from the ceiling to the floor.

"How did you know that was there?" you ask.

Olano shines his flashlight on a nearby wall. There is another drawing etched in the stone. "There's been a drawing by every booby trap in this place."

This third drawing shows a man standing in an enormous, open hand. The three of you review the three drawings quickly, trying to put the puzzle together as fast as you can. They've got to mean something: one man standing on another man's shoulders . . . a veil over the statue's eye . . . and finally, a man standing in a giant hand.

"They've got to be instructions!" you say. "Maybe how to operate the statue!"

"Maybe how *not* to operate the statue," Celeste says. "Don't forget, this place has more tricks than a magician's sleeve."

"There's only one way to find out," you say. "Let's get out of here and try it out on the statue."

"How do we get out of here?" Olano says.

"We could split up. Whoever gets outside to the statue first tries the three instructions," Celeste suggests.

"Let's go!" you say.

Splitting up has increased your chances of finding the right exit out of the maze and back to the entrance in the base of the statue. It's also lowered your chances against BRUTE. Twenty to one doesn't sound like very good odds in any game.

"Where is my mind?" you suddenly say out loud. "Olano! Celeste!" you call, but there is no answer and you hear no footsteps. You must have walked farther than you thought before you remembered — the statue has no hand to stand on. It doesn't have any arms at all! Those drawings are either a trap or a joke. You've got to warn the others just in case they haven't realized it yet.

You hold your breath — footsteps! They are quiet and slow at first. Then they stop, as though someone were listening. Then they begin again. You press yourself to the wall as tightly as you can. You're too tired to run. You're going to wait for your moment and jump whoever is coming.

The footsteps come closer. Twenty feet away . . . 10 feet away. You crouch, ready to spring and tackle a BRUTE agent at his knees. Before you leap, a light shines in your eyes. You don't hesitate. You just jump toward your attacker with a scream and the two of you roll around in the dirt struggling for each other's throats. But you're losing!

CHAPTER
15

"Get off me, you turkey," your attacker shouts at you. And you both start laughing.

"Olano, why didn't you say it was you?" you ask.

"You didn't give me much of a chance. What are you doing? Trying out for the Dallas Cowboys? I'm going to be sore for a month. I thought you were supposed to be sick," he says, rubbing his side.

"What are you doing here?" you ask.

"Looking for you. Orion, have you gone bananas? The statue doesn't have any arms *or* hands!" Olano says.

"I remembered that, too, and started to come looking for you," you say.

Suddenly Olano's hand is clamped over your mouth. "Shh," he whispers.

"Celeste," you whisper to Olano. "She's remembered it, too, by now."

"Yeah," Olano says.

"Psst! Celeste! Over here," you say.

A quick round of automatic rifle fire explodes in the dark, shells ricochet off the walls, and the noise is deafening.

"Mistake with a capital M," you shout.

You and Olano start running, with bullets chasing you, kicking up dirt at your heels. You're running so fast that you don't notice that there is someone standing directly in your escape route. The three of you collide and crash to the ground. You snap on the flashlight so you don't make the mistake of attacking Olano.

"The statue doesn't have any hands. Let's get our act together, guys," Celeste says.

"Okay, the drawings don't apply to the statue, but there's got to be something else here, some reason why people enter and never leave."

With BRUTE at your back, you travel in the dark as quietly as you can. But in the middle of a maze, your back soon becomes your side, then your front — where are you now? No matter what you do, you're bound to run into BRUTE again eventually.

"ACT agents, can you hear me?" It's the voice of Jack Assante. "We've found it. The professor was right on all counts. It is far more powerful than anything on Earth. If you want to see a demonstration, come on. Just follow the sound of my voice to the middle of the maze."

Do you have any choice? Wandering around the maze will get you nowhere. This is a situation that calls for face-to-face confrontation. So you walk forward, following the sound of Jack's laughter.

"Now!" he shouts. And before you can know what's going to happen, it happens — a quick, loud explosion and the corridor walls split into a thousand pieces. You dive for the ground and try to cover yourself from the flying rocks and dirt. When the smoke clears, your path forward is completely blocked by piles of stone and debris.

"They've sealed us out. We'll never get to the center of the maze," Celeste says.

"And we cannot escape," Olano says. "The temple will be our tomb. Chalk up one for the legends."

"Come on, don't give up yet, guys," you say. "We'll just go down one of them. Maybe there's another exit to the outside somewhere. Hey — wait! They haven't just sealed us out. They've sealed *themselves* in."

"Why would they do that?" Celeste asks, wiping at a cut on her forehead.

"That's the point. They wouldn't," you say. "They've got to get out of here somehow. So if there's a way for them to get out, then there's a way for us to get to them!"

"Maybe," Celeste says. "So do we split up again?"

"That didn't work out so well the last

time, if you don't mind some constructive criticism," Olano says.

Stepping over and around the ruins, you make your way through the maze. The dust aftershock from the explosion hasn't settled in this corridor yet. A stale, musty odor fills the chambers you pass through as you follow the paths.

"Stop pushing me. I'm going as fast as I can," you tell Olano.

"I didn't push you. You probably stumbled. I'm sure you could use some more medication by now," he says to you.

"Maybe the Devorim Force is beginning to get to you, too, because you keep pushing me and don't even know you're doing it," you say.

Olano lets the remark slide by. Instead he turns around and calls to Celeste, "We've got to hurry. Come on."

"Guys," Celeste says in a calm voice, "this is going to sound strange, but I can't move. My mind is telling my body to move, but something is holding me back."

You and Olano shine your lights at Celeste. She is standing by herself, pushing against the air and unable to move. Then you see the first one materialize. It swoops down from the ceiling and circles around Celeste before disappearing.

"What was that?" you and Celeste ask in unison. "It looked like a ghost. . . ."

"It looked like a Murzik warrior," Olano says. "Perhaps the fiercest of all the warrior tribes who ever lived in the Boranu. Of course, there haven't been any Murzik warriors in about 100 years."

More begin to appear. They are transparent people with human features, but bodies like cloudy soap bubbles.

"I think those explosions disturbed somebody's tomb," Olano says.

"Do you think they're unhappy about it?" you ask.

"They'll let us know if they are," Olano says.

"I don't believe this," Celeste says. "I spent months convincing my two-year-old that there are no such things as ghosts."

But the ghosts are right in front of your eyes. They fly around you, then through you. Every time you try to continue down the corridor, they try to block your way. They seem to be trying to tell you something. But is it: Don't go this way — there's a better way? Or: Don't go at all?

The ghosts lead you into a room in the temple sealed by a rotting wood door and thick layers of cobwebs. They both give way with a minimal push.

"What kind of room is this?" you ask Olano, hoping that there is something familiar to him, some kind of clue to why the ghosts directed you here.

"The gym?" he says with a shrug. "I've never seen anything like it before."

"The civilization that built the temple and the power source may have been from another planet," Celeste reminds you. "There's no reason why any of this should be recognizable."

But there's got to be some kind of clue here, even in this empty, cavernous room. Just then your light beam hits one of the walls. Your eyes widen and your mouth falls open. You can barely tell your companions to come see the hideous pictures you've discovered.

"Oh, no. It's too awful," Celeste says, looking at the scenes of hideous torture.

"The paintings on the walls must be a history of the alien civilization on Earth," Olano says.

"What kind of people would do these horrible things? How could they?" you say.

"They were monsters," Olano answers.

"Of unmatched cruelty," Celeste says, finishing his sentence. "I've seen enough."

"I guess that answers our questions about whatever is waiting for us in the middle of the maze," you say. "We must destroy it before BRUTE destroys the world with it."

CHAPTER

16

What if Jack Assante and the other BRUTE agents have already figured out how to use the idol's power source? What if they are just waiting around for you to walk in because they need a test guinea pig or three? What if they have already left with it and sent their threatening messages to the heads of every government in the world? What if . . . what if . . . what if. . . .

"We've done the best we can," Olano says to you as you walk the final twists of the maze.

"How did you know what I was thinking?" you ask.

"Because we're all thinking the same thing," Celeste says.

"Look — here we are," Olano says, and the three of you stop still in your tracks.

In the center of the maze you have come

to a large room with tall walls and golden doors that reach all the way to the ceiling. On the doors is the symbol of this evil alien race, the statue with the large eye. You can't see through the crack in the doors, but you can hear voices inside and one of them is Jack Assante's. He seems to be talking excitedly to someone over a radio. So you figure that BRUTE has brought a transmitter with them so that all the orders could come down from the top.

You quietly open the doors and step in. All those in the room have their backs to the door. They either aren't expecting you or are just too busy to notice. This may be your chance!

Then from behind, you hear the unmistakable sound of an automatic rifle being cocked and readied. The barrel of the rifle prods each of you on the back of your necks. And you march forward obediently. Now Jack Assante turns around and he is clearly surprised to see you.

"Well, come on in," he says, quickly putting his grin back on his face. "I can't honestly say that I've been expecting you, but it's nice to see familiar faces. You guys are good, really good."

"We don't like to leave a mission half finished," you say.

"Kid, this mission is finished as far as you're concerned," Jack says to you, taking a

96

revolver out of the holster he now wears. "But you probably want to see what all the fuss was about. Come with me."

You follow him, and the BRUTE agent with the rifle stays reluctantly behind. You can tell immediately that Jack is leading you to a source of the Devorim Force stronger than you have felt the entire mission. Laughing, he leads you into the next room. Like the previous room, this one is almost empty. But this room has in it the last thing in the world you expected to see!

In the middle, on a stone pedestal, is another statue, the same as the one outside, only larger, shinier, and with an enormous red eye in the middle of the face. And this one has an enormous hand at the end of a long, outstretched arm. The pieces of the puzzle begin to fit together.

"My readings indicate this is the primary source of energy, the one that's been giving us the fantastic readings all the way back in the United States," Jack says, walking around the statue. His revolver never leaves his hand and sometimes he points with it as though it were just another finger. "My best guess is that old fool Ballaster did something to set this thing off or warm it up or something like that. Whatever he did, it was enough to convince him of the power this statue has. Then he came crying to ACT for help. Ballaster had no imagination."

"Are you saying you haven't figured out how the statue works yet?" Celeste asks. She is walking around the statue, examining it from every side. Jack Assante keeps his eye and his revolver trained on her.

"Yeah, we think we've got it figured out," Jack says.

"That's a lie," Celeste snaps.

"Good for you," Olano says.

"Keep quiet unless you're real anxious to meet your ancestors," Jack says. "You're the nuclear expert, Celeste. Do you know how it works?"

"We know too much about it, Assante," she says.

"Look, you can't frighten me; you can't change my mind; you can't buy me off. So let's cool it with those corny ACT agent games, okay? You'll live longer — not a lot longer, but longer."

"Celeste is trying to tell you that we've found out a lot about the civilization that built these statues. They were terrible people," you say.

"I'm no Boy Scout myself," Jack says. "Just show me the on/off switch, got it?"

"This probably isn't just an energy source," you keep arguing. "It's probably some kind of destructive weapon."

"Kid, you've been playing Space Invaders too long. I'm not looking for something that will automatically turn on my toaster when I walk in the door. I'm here because we had every finger we could find crossed, hoping we could use this as a weapon.''

''We can't help you. We don't know how it operates,'' Olano says.

Jack comes up and sticks his revolver in Olano's chest. ''Are you telling me that you don't know how to work this statue?''

''That's what I'm telling you,'' Olano says, staring Jack directly in the eyes.

''Okay, now we're getting somewhere,'' Jack says, moving back. ''Now I know I don't need you for anything. I can kill you any time I want. How about you, Celeste? Are you going to tell me something I want to hear?''

''No can do. I accepted this mission for better or for worse,'' Celeste says.

''Till death do you part,'' Jack says. ''Okay, we're cutting down on a lot of excess baggage here. Your turn, computer genius. You must be feeling pretty sick by now after all this exposure to these substances from outer space. And I've got a brand-new bottle of little green pills in the other room, Orion. What do you say?''

''Swallow it,'' you say.

''You are dead meat, Orion. Do you have a smart remark for that?'' Jack snaps back.

Just then another BRUTE agent enters the room and whispers something in Jack's ear. Jack smiles and shakes his head. ''Okay, we've found a third drawing on the wall. I think if we put the three together, we're going to see some fireworks. Have a seat by the wall over there, you three," he says to you. Then he starts ordering the other agents around. "Hank, call Control and tell them we're about ready to light the candle. Larry, you and Rivera do the climbing when I give you the signal."

Then Jack turns back to you. "Maybe you had the three clues, but we had the right statue. With or without your help, as you can see, we're going to try this baby out."

"Jack," a BRUTE agent calls from the other room, "Control says Happy Birthday, now light the candle."

"Go for it," Jack says with a smile.

CHAPTER
17

You watch silently, but with a creeping fear throughout your body. Two BRUTE agents begin to act out the drawings you found on the walls of the temple maze. First, one agent climbs on the shoulders of the other. By stretching as far as he can, the agent on top can reach the large gold hand of the statue. He pulls himself up into the hand and turns to wait for Jack's next signal.

"Don't do it, Jack," you shout.

The man in the statue's hand looks at you for a second, but when Jack makes a motion with his revolver, the agent turns around, stretches up, and removes an opalescent headpiece covering the eye of the statue. The statue's red eye immediately starts to glow.

"Okay," Jack says, standing by you, "I think you've seen enough. Don't want you to see the whole show. Who wants to die first?"

With that he cocks his revolver into the ready position. But something makes him stop. It's nothing you can see. It starts out as something you feel, a low rumbling in the floor and walls. Everyone is looking around for an explanation. The rumbling gets louder and now you can hear it as well as feel it.

"Look at the eye," Celeste says. "It's glowing brighter now!"

"It's the ceiling!" you shout. You look up and a section of the massive stone ceiling is slowly grinding back. Small stones are falling from the roof to the floor. Sunlight begins to break through the dust from the moving stone.

"There's the other idol! We're right beneath it," you say, pointing at the growing hole in the ceiling.

The two statues begin to rotate slowly, as the low rumbling becomes a louder humming. The floor and walls are vibrating now, but that's only the beginning. Jack moves away from you to be closer to the statue with the red eye. He, too, is looking up at the idol outside as it rotates in line with the statue below.

Finally the two statues stop their rotation. They are in exactly the same position. You hold your breath as a beam of light shoots through the clear lens of the idol above and straight down to the red lens of the idol below. The red lens turns a fiery red and begins to blink.

What's wrong with everyone? We should

be running, you think. You wonder if this is how it feels to be caught on a railroad track. You know you should run, but you want to know what it's like when that train is on its way.

Just then the statue's red eye stops pulsing and spits out a continuous, deadly beam of light. And the BRUTE agent who was standing on the statue's hand isn't there anymore. He isn't anywhere. The beam swings in an ever-widening arc and picks off another agent. He disappears, too.

Jack tries to run out the door. He is the third victim. Running at top speed one second — then gone the next split instant.

"Lasers?" Olano asks Celeste.

"Not anything I've seen before," she says. "Move into that corner. We've got to stay out of its path."

The horrible statue continues to rotate and the remaining BRUTE agents who have run into the room disappear without a scream or a trace left behind.

"We've got to do something!" you say.

"What?" Olano says. "How can we destroy it?"

"There's only one way," Celeste says. "Give it a taste of its own medicine."

"What do you mean?" Olano asks.

"The only thing powerful enough to destroy this statue is the statue itself. We've got to deflect the beam back at the statue. Unfortunately, I don't have a mirror with me,"

Celeste says. "It's the last thing in the world I thought I'd need."

You aren't listening to Olano or Celeste as carefully as you should, because you've been watching the idol's actions. The deadly beam is making a complete circle, firing a continuous deadly light down at the floor.

"If we move, it will get us," Celeste says.

"If we sit here, it will get us," Olano says.

Your response is to pull out your computer.

"About how high is the idol's eye?" you demand of anyone who will answer.

"Who knows?! What are you doing?" Olano yells, terrified.

"Getting the angle right," you say. "I've got to figure out exactly the angle from the floor to the idol's eye."

"I'd say it's 22 feet to the center of the lens," Celeste estimates. "And 11 feet to its heart. Is that what you're looking for, Orion?"

"Exactly," you reply, doing some quick calculations. "And how far are we from the base?"

"About 15 feet, I'd say."

Type this program into your computer, but don't run it yet. Lines 50, 70, 100, 220, and 240 should each be typed as one line on your computer.

PROGRAM 5

```
10  REM BEAM DEFLECTOR
20  PI = 3.14159
30  PRINT "HOW HIGH IS THE IDOL'S EYE";
40  INPUT Y1
50  PRINT "HOW HIGH IS THE IDOL'S
    HEART";
60  INPUT Y2
70  PRINT "HOW FAR ARE YOU FROM THE
    IDOL'S BASE";
80  INPUT X
90  W = INT(RND(1) * 4) + 2
100 PRINT "WHAT ANGLE (IN DEGREES) WILL
    YOU SET THE MIRROR?"
110 INPUT Z
120 A = ATN(Y2/X)
130 B = ATN(Y1/X)
140 B2 = (B-A)/2
150 C = PI/2 - B2
160 D = PI-B-C
170 D = D*(180/PI)
180 PRINT
190 IF ABS(D-Z)>W THEN 220
200 PRINT "*** THE IDOL IS DESTROYED!!***"
210 END
220 PRINT "YOU MISSED BY ";
    INT (ABS(D-Z));" DEGREES"
230 PRINT
240 PRINT "IF YOU ARE STILL ALIVE, TRY
    AGAIN"
250 PRINT
260 GOTO 100
```

IBM	Apple		Radio Shack		Commodore		TI	Atari
PC & PCjr	II+	IIe	TRS-80	Color	64	VIC-20	99/4A	400/800
	✓	✓		✓	✓	✓		

This program will run on all personal computers in the chart above. See the Reference Manual, page 125, for changes for other micros.

"Okay, I've got it!" you say and stand up quickly.

"No! Come back," Celeste cries.

"You'll be killed!" Olano shouts above the noise of the beam.

"No, I won't," you answer. "I just remembered — I can't be killed!"

CHAPTER

18

The laserlike beam from the eye is burning into the floor, since there are no more BRUTE agents to disintegrate. You walk up to the spot where it will be in 20 seconds. That isn't much time, but it's time enough to calculate again the angle of deflection you need. Quickly you remove Olano's necklace from your neck and smile to yourself. He said no matter what happened, this necklace would make sure that you'd be around to tell the story. Well, if this little trick works, you'll all be around to tell the story — but you'll bet no one believes you. The eye is wreaking its vengeance on the floor, and in four seconds it will sweep over you. You carefully lean the shiny, round, silver pendant of the necklace on the floor, at what you think is the right angle. And then you run like crazy.

"Let's get out of here!" you shout as the three of you make your break for the doorway. "Hold on to your Richter scales. This should be a beauty!"

Run the program NOW! Input the measurements Celeste gave. You will have to guess at what angle to set the mirror.

Buzzzzz!! The sound of the statue spitting its laser bullet is followed by the largest explosion you've ever heard. It lifts you off the floor and the entire temple trembles and rumbles — more explosions and blinding light from the other room. Then pieces of the idol outside fall into the room below and the explosions continue. It's like being in the middle of an enormous skyrocket!

The silence afterward is just as earthshaking as the deafening explosions were. When the three of you return to the statue room, you are only a little surprised by what you see. The room is empty. There is no rubble or debris. Both statues are gone without a trace. Olano's beautiful necklace is gone as well. However, for the first time in two days, you feel like your old self again. Not a trace of the Devorim Force remains.

EPILOGUE

Half a day later you are half the world away — back in ACT headquarters explaining the results of your mission to Mark Huntington, the coordinator for the mission.

"We knew it was going to be a difficult assignment. We didn't know it was going to be so costly. We lost two good agents, agents Erda and Digger," Huntington says. "And, of course, we lost Professor Ballaster. He never lived to see the world cheer him — or condemn him — for his discovery of the temple."

"What kind of energy readings did we get the day of the explosions?" Celeste asks.

"Astronomical," the coordinator replies. "You must be right about the two idols, Celeste. The first one was an energy source of its own, all right. But its principal job was to feed light to the lower and larger eye. What kind of energy source it was and what kind of weapon it was used for, I guess we'll never know.

"Well, our archaelogists are climbing all over that temple by this time. They'll get enough information about that alien civilization to keep them arguing for years. You completed a good mission, team. You deserve some rest — get some! We may need you again at any minute."

Outside Huntington's office, you say your good-byes. Celeste is off to pick up her daughter.

"I'm going back to Purdue. Final exams are coming up," Olano says. "And after graduation, maybe I'll go back to the Boranu. What about you, Orion?"

"I've got to go home and study for a chemistry test and wait for another alert," you say. The three of you shake hands. And hope that you'll meet again.

Monday afternoon. School is out. Still bleary-eyed, you're heading for your locker and a little fresh air. You stop dead in your tracks. Taped to the outside of your locker is a red envelope!

"No — no, it can't be. Oh, no!" you say.

"What's the matter with you?" asks Cindy Grossman, the girl with the locker next to yours. "If you don't want my valentine, I'll take it back, okay? Sometimes you're really weird, you know?"

"Yeah, I know," you say. "Thanks for the card, Cindy. I had a tough weekend."

REFERENCE
MANUAL

Note to User: The programming activities in this book have been designed for use with the BASIC programming language on the IBM PC, PCjr, Apple II Plus or Apple IIe (with Applesoft BASIC), Commodore 64, Vic-20, TI 99/4A, Atari 400/800, Radio Shack TRS-80 Level 2 or greater, and the Radio Shack Color Computer. Each machine has its own operating procedures for starting up BASIC. So make sure you're in BASIC before trying to run any of these programs.*

The version of the program included in the text will run on most of the computers listed above. However, a few of the commands used are not available on some home systems. If the program as given does not run on one of the micros listed above, modification instructions will be included in this reference manual.

---

*Also make sure you type NEW before entering each program to clear out any leftovers from previous activities.

TI 99/4A users, please note: The Texas Instruments version of regular BASIC doesn't allow multiple statements on a line or the word GOTO following a THEN. Multiple statements on the same line should be entered as one statement per line number and any THEN GOTO line number should be entered as just a THEN line number.

Even if you're using a computer other than the ones mentioned, the programs may still work, since they are always written in the most general BASIC.

If you need help with one of the computer activities in the *Micro Adventure,* or want to understand how a program works, you'll find what you need in this manual.

Naturally, programs must be typed into your computer *exactly* as given. If the program should run on your computer but you're having problems, do a list on the program and check your typing before you try anything else. Even a misplaced comma or space might cause an error of syntax that will prevent the whole program from working.

TERMS YOU NEED TO KNOW

Computer experts use a special "language" when talking about programs. Here are some common terms that will help you understand the explanations in this manual.

Arrays are groups of two or more logically related data elements in a program that have the same name. However, so that the individual elements in the array can be used, each is also identified by its own address (called an *index* by programmers). You can think of an array as an apartment building. One hundred people might live at the Northwest Apartments (or 100 pieces of information might be stored in the NW Array). But each unit within the building has a number (like Apt 14), so that it can be located and receive mail. In the NW Array, 14 could be the index to find a particular piece of information, and would be written NW (14). If you put the 26 letters of the alphabet into an array called Alpha, then Alpha (2) would equal B because B is the second letter of the alphabet.

ASCII (pronounced *asskee)* is the standard code used by most microcomputers to represent characters such as letters, numbers, and punctuation.

ASC is a function in BASIC that will supply a character's ASCII code. For example, ASC (''A'') will give you the number 65.

Bugs are errors or mistakes in a program that keep it from doing what it's supposed to do. Some of the programming activities in this book will ask you to find and fix a bug so that the program will work correctly.

Functions are ready-made routines that perform standard calculations in a program. It's sort of like having a key on a calculator that computes a square root or the cosine of a number. The programming language BASIC comes with a number of standard functions to perform certain tasks. For example, the function SQR (x) will find the square root of any number when x is replaced by that number. You might want to check the BASIC manual that came with your computer to see which functions are available on your system.

INT is a function that changes any number that you supply into a whole number or integer. For example INT(4.5) will return the value 4. For numbers greater than 0, INT just throws away any fractions and supplies you with the whole number.

Loops are sections of programs that may be repeated more than once — usually a specified number of times, or until certain conditions are met. For example, if you wanted to write a program that would count from 1 to 100, a loop could be used to keep adding 1 to a counter variable until the number 100 was reached. Loops are most commonly formed with FOR/NEXT statements or GOTO commands.

You'll find many examples of these in the programs in this book.

Random Number Generator   This function, which is called RND in BASIC, lets you generate numbers at "random" just as though you were throwing a set of dice and didn't know which number was going to come up next. In most home computers, the RND function returns a fraction between 0 and 1. To get numbers in a larger range, the program must multiply the fraction by a larger number. For example, RND * 10 will produce numbers between 0 and 10.

REM   This command is used to tell the computer that whatever is on a particular line is just a comment or a remark and should not be executed. An example might look like this:

10 REM THIS PROGRAM COUNTS DOWN.

Variables are names used to represent values that will change during the course of a program. For example, a variable named D$ might represent any day of the week. It may help you to think of a variable as a storage box, waiting to receive whatever information you want to put in. Variables that deal with strings of characters are always followed by a dollar sign. Variables that end in a percent sign always hold integers (whole numbers like 1, 2, 3, 500). Variables with a pound sign or no special

115

character at the end hold numbers that may
contain fractions. The number of characters allowed in a variable name varies from computer
to computer.

PROGRAM 1: THE DECODER

Modifications for Other Micros

TI 99/4A — The TI uses SEG$ to get a part of
a string instead of MID$. It works the same
way.
```
100 I$ = SEG$(C$,I,1)
120 P$ = P$ & I$
170 K = ASC(SEG$(K$,J,1)) - ASC("A") + 1
220 P$ = P$ & CHR$(P + ASC("A") - 1)
```

Atari 400/800 — The Atari handles strings dif-
ferently than most other microcomputers. Add
this line to encoder or decoder program after
line 10:
```
 11 DIM K$(10),C$(255),P$(255),I$(1)
```

and change the following lines:
```
100 I$ = C$(I,I)
120 P$(LEN(P$) + 1) = I$
170 K = ASC(K$(J,J)) - ASC("A") + 1
220 P$(LEN(P$) + 1) = CHR$(P + ASC
    ("A") - 1)
```

What the Program Does

  Orion uses this program to decode the
message from ACT.

How the Program Works

This decoder program uses a key to decode the secret message. A "key" is a special word that tells the program just how to decode each letter of a message.

To encode the message we use a formula like this:

Key = TOPAZ msg = THIS IS YOUR MISSION

Formula:

```
 TOPA ZT OPAZ     TOPAZTO  Key
—THIS IS YOUR     MISSION—Text
```

```
 ZGGH QA PAFH     GFWHQEA
```
(the encoded message)

The way the program works, the key is always the sum of the values of the two other letters.

One of the letters is the plaintext; the other is the encoded letter. The computer must deal with letters as numbers. So we tell it to add or subtract the ASCII values by using the ASC function.

Here's something really interesting about this program. It can *encode* your messages as well as *decode* them. This may seem a bit magical, but the reason is that we always get the key when we add the encoded letter to the plaintext number. That means that to get the missing letter, either plaintext or "cipher," we just subtract the "letter" we *do* know from the key. (Yes, this is algebra!)

This means that it isn't enough to have the program to decode a message; you must also have the "key" or password. BRUTE will have to do more than steal the computer to break ACT's secret message this time!

PROGRAM 2: THE ANALYSIS

Modifications for Other Micros

Atari 400/800 — Don't use quotes in your data statements. The Atari BASIC includes them in the string, and that's not what we want for this program. Make these changes:

```
 50  DATA RETRIUM.,HYDROGEN
 60  DATA DELIOS..,XENON...,RADON...
100  INPUT Z:A(I)=Z
```

And add:

```
 15  DIM B$(20),N$(20),Y$(5)
```

TI99/4A — Make these changes:

```
230  IF C < = 5 THEN 240
235  GOSUB 340
```

What the Program Does

Orion uses this program to analyze the results of data about some element readings. The program will graphically display the results. You enter the data at the keyboard for each of the readings. The names of the elements are in DATA statements in lines 50 and 60.

How the Program Works

At line 120 we RESTORE the data. This means that the next time we READ data, the program will start at the beginning of the data all over again.

Lines 160 through 250 are in a loop that processes the data.

At line 170, an element name is read, and then goes into the string variable B$. Each time we reach this statement in the loop, the next name value from the DATA statements is placed into this variable.

Line 180 performs the math-magics of this program. It uses two mathematical functions. The ABS function is used to make sure that any number that is returned is greater than or equal to 0. ABS(-2) comes back as $+2$ and ABS($+2$) also comes back as $+2$ and so forth. The SIN function returns the SINE of a value in RADIANS. Radians are units (something like degrees) for measuring how wide an angle is. The SINE is used in trigonometry, and is a ratio between sides of a triangle. Your math teacher can explain the details.

After printing the asterisks, we ask whether you want to see if the danger level has exceeded certain bounds. If it has, we want to warn Orion about the danger! This check takes place at line 370. The program uses the level to warn Orion of how bad the threat is.

That's all there is to it. Try changing the

values of the element readings and see how the
graph changes.

PROGRAM 3: THE IDOL'S EYE

Modifications for Other Micros

IBM-PC — Make these changes:

```
 30 CLS
260 LOCATE V,H
420 LOCATE 20,1:END
```

VIC-20 and Commodore-64 —
Make these changes:

```
15 V$="CLR/HME↓↓↓↓↓↓↓↓↓↓↓↓↓
    ↓↓↓↓↓↓↓↓↓↓↓"
30 PRINT "SHIFT-CLR/HOME"
```
(*Note:* This is the SHIFTED CLR/HOME KEY)
```
260 PRINT LEFT$(V$,V);TAB(H);
420 PRINT LEFT$(V$,20):END
```

TRS-80 — Make these changes:

```
 30 CLS
260 PRINT@((H−1)*64+H);
420 PRINT@1152:END
```

Radio Shack Color Computer — Make these
changes:

```
 30 CLS
260 PRINT@((H−1)*32+H);
420 PRINT@640:END
```

Atari 400/800 — Make these changes:

```
11 DIM O$(6),B$(6),C$(6),S$(6),G$(6)
30 GRAPHICS 0
```

```
  60 READ P: P(I)=P
 260 POSITION H,V
 310 PRINT S$(1,N);
 330 PRINT G$(1,G);
 350 PRINT S$(1,N);
 420 POSITION 1,20 : END
```

TI-99/4A — Full program below:

```
 10 REM THE IDOL'S EYE
 20 DIM U(5)
 30 CALL CLEAR
 50 DATA 4,5,6,6,5
 60 FOR I=1 TO 5
 70 READ U(I)
 80 NEXT I
 90 Q=ASC("  ")
100 B=ASC("@")
110 C=ASC("*")
120 FOR I=1 TO 3
130 FOR J=1 TO 12
140 V=J
150 IF I<>3 THEN 170
160 V=13-V
170 S=Q
180 G=C
190 IF I<>2 THEN 220
200 S=B
210 G=B
220 L=20-2*ABS(6-V)
230 IF V<=6 THEN 250
240 L=L+2
250 H=7-V
260 IF V<=6 THEN 280
```

```
270 H = V − 6
280 CALL HCHAR(V + 5,H + 5,C,2)
290 N = U(6 − H)
300 G1 = L − 2*N − 4
310 IF G1 > = 0 THEN 330
320 G1 = 0
330 CALL HCHAR(V + 5,H + 7,S,N)
340 IF G1 = 0 THEN 360
350 CALL HCHAR(V + 5,H + 7 + N,G,G1)
360 CALL HCHAR(V + 5,H + 7 + N + G1,S,N)
370 CALL
    HCHAR(V + 5,H + 7 + N + G1 + N,C,2)
380 NEXT J
390 FOR W = 1 to 500
400 NEXT W
410 NEXT I
420 END
```

What the Program Does

This program makes a picture of the idol's eye and even makes it blink!

How the Program Works

The eye is made up of 12 "lines" on the screen. There are three parts to the program: 1. *draw* the eye; 2. *close* the eyelid; and 3. *open* the eyelid. These steps are controlled by two FOR:NEXT loops. Find them in the program.

There is one more thing to notice about the eye. If you draw a cross through it (split it in half up and down and across), each quarter is just like another, maybe turned around a bit or as a mirror image. The eye is symmetrical. The program uses this fact to use only enough data to describe one quarter of the eye, and figures the rest out from that.

By knowing which line it is on (the variable V) it can figure out how long the line is supposed to be. That is put into L. It also can figure out how far in it has to go before starting to draw its asterisks on each line (variable H).

Having this all figured out, the program can print the eye. It prints two asterisks on each line, followed by the number of spaces in the "white" of the eye (that's what is in the DATA statement), followed by the pupil of the eye, the other part of the white of the eye, and two more asterisks to outline the eye. When the eye blinks, we just substitute all @s for the white of the eye and the pupil.

PROGRAM 4: THE MAZE

Modifications for Other Micros

Atari — Add:
```
15 DIM Q$(1)
```
Change:
```
30  DATA N,S,E,W
    (leave out the quotation marks.)
40  FOR I=1 TO 4:READ Q$:C$(I)=
    Q$:NEXT I
```

```
140  INPUT T:A1(I)=T
230  PRINT B;C$(X+1,X+1);" ";
```

What the Program Does

ACT members discovered four entrances to underground passages. Above each entrance are a lot of numbers that you figure are the key to the passageways. The chief could tell you only that of the four paths, the only one that leads to the idol's secret leads back to the same spot in the cave. You enter the numbers from above the passage entrances to determine which passage is a full circle. Each entrance has nine numbers above it.

How the Program Works

Line 120 reads in the nine numbers for each passage. You type the numbers in. Each number describes a distance and a direction.

It works this way: Using the values on the compass for the four directions, you divide by four to get the distance (at line 200) and take the remainder to give you the direction (line 210). The distance is kept in B and the direction in X. The total north, south, east, and west is added up in line 220 and stored in the right place in the array P. P(0) holds the total of all the north distances, P(1) the south distances, P(2) the east distances, and P(3) the west distances. We know that we have come full circle when the north and south distances, and the east and west distances, are equal.

PROGRAM 5: BEAM DEFLECTOR

Modifications for Other Micros

Atari — Make this change:
90 W = INT(RND(0)*4)+2

Radio Shack — Make this change:
90 W = RND(4)+2

IBM — Make this change:
15 RANDOMIZE
90 W = INT(RND*4)+2

TI-99/4A — Make this change:
15 RANDOMIZE
90 W = INT(RND*4) + 2

What the Program Does

This is the program Orion uses to place the mirror so that it will deflect the beam of energy from the idol.

There's a lot of math involved in this program. We aren't about to put your math teacher out of a job by trying to explain it to you in two paragraphs. It all has to do with geometry and such. It uses the ATN function. The ATN function gives us the "arctangent." That's an angle measure in *radians*. To use the function, we use the ratio of two sides of a triangle. We use the ATN function twice.

The first triangle is the one from the idol's eye, to the idol's base, to where the mirror is. The second triangle is from the idol's heart, to the idol's base, to where the mirror is.

Do you see where the ATN function is used? Can you find which variable is used to store the idol's height? Its heart?

By using the angles we have calculated with the ATN function, and knowing two other facts, we are able to figure out all the rest of the information we need to solve the problem. Those two facts are:

1. The angle of incidence equals the angle of reflection when light strikes a mirror.

2. There are 180 degrees, or PI radians, in a triangle.

Radians and degrees are both used to measure angles. Computers usually use radians. A lot of people use degrees. You can see how to convert radians to degrees in line 170. Can you guess how it is done? *Right!* Just multiply the number of radians by 180/PI. (PI is about 3.14159.)

Line 170 is where we get our final result, in degrees.

Look back at line 90. We use a RANDOM function here to make the problem a little trickier. After all, the idol is becoming rather unstable and shaky. We got a value from 1 to 7 at line 90. The angle you set the mirror at must come within that "random" number of degrees of the real value to kill the idol. That is checked in line 190.